Praise for other Don Strachey novels

"Lively, skillful...highly recommended."

The New York Times on *On the Other Hand, Death*

"As much travel memoir as mystery, this tenth in a series spanning three decades is supremely satisfying as both."

Bookmarks on *The 38 Million Dollar Smile*

"As always with the Strachey novels, the murder and mayhem takes a back seat to the keen social criticism and defiant wit of our detective."

Maureen Corrigan of NPR,
naming *Death Vows* one of the top five mysteries of 2008

"A gripping, fast-paced mystery."

Booklist on *Strachey's Folly*

"Stevenson's mysteries are among the wittiest and most politically pointed around."

The Washington Post on *Chain of Fools*

Featuring a roll call of some of the best writers of gay erotica and mysteries today!

M. Jules Aedin

Maura Anderson

Victor J. Banis

Jeanne Barrack

Laura Baumbach

Alex Beecroft

Sarah Black

Ally Blue

J.P. Bowie

Michael Breyette

P..A. Brown

Brenda Bryce

Jade Buchanan

James Buchanan

Charlie Cochrane

Kirby Crow

Dick D.

Ethan Day

Jason Edding

Angela Fiddler

Dakota Flint

S.J. Frost

Kimberly Gardner

Roland Graeme

Storm Grant

Amber Green

LB Gregg

Drewey Wayne Gunn

David Juhren

Samantha Kane

Kiernan Kelly

J.L. Langley

Josh Lanyon

Clare London

William Maltese

Gary Martine

Z.A. Maxfield

Patric Michael

AKM Miles

Jet Mykles

Willa Okati

L. Picaro

Neil Plakcy

Jordan Castillo Price

Luisa Prieto

Rick R. Reed

A.M. Riley

George Seaton

Jardonn Smith

Caro Soles

JoAnne Soper-Cook

Richard Stevenson

Clare Thompson

Lex Valentine

Stevie Woods

Check out titles, both available and forthcoming, at
www.mlrpress.com

COCKEYED

A Donald Strachey Mystery

RICHARD STEVENSON

mlrpress
www.mlrpress.com

Copyright 2010 by Richard Stevenson

Published by
MLR Press, LLC
3052 Gaines Waterport Rd.
Albion, NY 14411

Visit ManLoveRomance Press, LLC on the Internet:
www.mlrpress.com

Cover Art by Deana C. Jamroz
Editing by Judith David

ISBN# 978-1-60820-096-2

Issued 2010

"There's a lot to be said for making people laugh. Did you know that that's all some people have? It isn't much, but it's better than nothing in this cockeyed caravan."

Joel McCrea as movie director John L. Sullivan in Preston Sturges's *Sullivan's Travels* (1941)

CHAPTER ONE

The first time I laid eyes on Art Malanowski and Hunny Van Horn was the day Hunny won the first New York Lottery payout of one billion dollars.

Normally Timothy Callahan and I are settled in bed and ready to be cheered up by Jon Stewart at eleven, and then we try to stay awake for Colbert. But a colleague of Timmy's in Assemblyman Lipshutz's office phoned earlier and urged Timmy to catch the Channel 13 news at eleven. He said, "You've gotta see this to believe it," but refused to say what *it* was.

So we tuned in, and even before Hunny spoke, I said, "I do believe I detect what Johnny Carson used to call *a hint of mint.*"

"And then Ed would guffaw and say, 'I'm not touching that one with a ten-foot pole!'"

"And Johnny would get that look, and say, 'Mmmnn, a ten-foot pole!'"

"And the audience would crack up."

I said, "Don't you miss those days?"

"Nah."

A female reporter looking fresh out of communications school was doing a live stand-up outside Art and Hunny's house on Moth Street in Albany's North End. With its tar-paper-shingled front porch and aluminum awnings on the two second-story windows, Art and Hunny's place looked a good deal less minty than Timmy's and my Crow Street townhouse, with its Albany Historical Society bronze plaque next to the front door and the discreet rainbow stickers on half the Toyotas and Subaru Outbacks parked legally up and down the block. But the house on the television screen was in the old working-class North End, where predictability was harder to come by.

Huntington Van Horn, the reporter was saying, was the man who had purchased the unprecedentedly lucky winning ticket at DeMaestri's Variety Store, two blocks down the street at the corner of Moth and Transformer. Hunny was sharing his spectacular winnings, the young woman said with a smile, with his "longtime partner," Art.

"It's good," Timmy said, "that Albany TV reporters no longer refer to people like these two guys as admitted homosexuals. Of course, by the looks of Hunny and Art, they would have a tough time denying it."

As the reporter went on to describe how the August twelfth drawing was the State Lottery's first *Instant Warren* — making some fortunate player a Warren Buffet-like billionaire overnight —the picture showed Hunny and Art earlier inside their house. They were leaping about and flapping their wrists, shrieking with joy, uncorking champagne bottles and exchanging air kisses with others in the room. One of the celebrants was a middle-aged black man with large breasts, a heavy beard and a single rhinestone-studded earring dangling from his left earlobe and extending down to just above his collarbone. On this spectacularly lucky day, could the sparklers have been actual diamonds? Also prominent in the party crowd were two identical, nicely sculpted Caucasian youths of about community college age on whose T-shirts were printed the words WANT SOME?

We soon saw more tape of lottery officials earlier in the evening exclaiming over the Instant Warren drawing, and reporting that ticket sales were the heaviest in the lottery's history, and going on about how beneficial the lottery was for state educational programs. Then we were back live with the reporter. She was up on the front porch now and moving determinedly past the porch swing and through the open front door to the scene of festive mayhem in the Malanowski-Van Horn living room.

It was a little hard to hear the reporter over the Village People's "In the Navy" blasting from somewhere outside camera range, but it was apparent that she was moving toward the man of the hour, who was now at the center of an undulating and somewhat disheveled all-male kick line. With their arms draped over one another's shoulders, the dancers were having trouble keeping their champagne in their glasses, and some of the bubbly splashed onto the well-groomed reporter as she approached Hunny.

He was a short stout man, about sixty, I guessed, with a frizz of gray-blond hair around a bare pate that glistened in the TV lights. Hunny's pale blue eyes were bright with merriment, and there were two smiles on his blocky face, a broad one of his own, and the other the scarlet imprint on his right cheek of an apparent congratulatory smooch from somebody who was wearing lipstick. Hunny had on dark jeans that looked brand new, a caftan-like lavender shirt and a blingy gold-colored amulet on a necklace that looked phallic but could have been a doggie treat or a cucumber from the damaged-farm-produce bin.

As the reporter closed in on Hunny, he spotted her moving toward him and broke away from the kick line and, in instant full Norma Desmond mode, came vamping at the camera, intoning tragically, "I am ready for my *clooose*-up, Channel 13!"

The room erupted in hilarity, and the reporter smiled agreeably, if maybe not quite getting the joke.

Riveted, Timmy said, "There we are. Our people. We're on TV. But I don't see Gore Vidal anywhere."

"Or Eleanor Roosevelt. I hope straight viewers don't get the wrong idea."

Now the reporter was yelling into Hunny's ear, "So how does it feel, Hunny? Being the state's first lottery billionaire?"

Grabbing the mike, Hunny shrieked into it, "Oh, girl! How do I *feel*? I feel like I just had a date with…oh, who's that hot number who almost won *American Idol*?"

Somebody in the room yelled, "Susan Boyle!" This brought down the house with cackles and groans.

"Listen, girl," Hunny said, "I have to tell you, I just feel like the luckiest old queen in Albany, that's how I feel. I would have been floating on air just to win a thousand dollars, which would have been really in*cred*ible. But to win a *million* dollars is just…it just doesn't seem real!"

"Billion!" several voices shouted out, and Hunny did a take and clutched his chest and faked a heart attack.

"God, I'm richer than Madonna," Hunny blurted out, recovering, and then was struck by another sudden thought and cried, "Oh, Madonna, honey, I'm sorry, I'm sorry, I didn't mean that! Girl, *nobody* is richer than you are! If you're watching, I'm still your slave, and even if I'm almost a rich as you are now, I'll never be as *fabulous* as you are!"

This produced gales of laughter, as well of cries of "That's for sure!" and "Yes, you are! Yes, you are!"

Still mesmerized, Timmy said, "Oh my."

I shared his amazement. "This will go down in the annals of Albany television news."

As somebody passed Hunny a cigarette, and a hand with a lighter appeared from off-camera and lit it for him, the reporter asked, "What are your plans for your fantastic winnings, Hunny? And what about work from now on? Are you planning on keeping your job at BJ's Warehouse?"

Spraying smoke and droplets of champagne at the reporter, Hunny yelped, "Girl, are you kidding? I'll miss all my friends at BJ's. In fact, I'll probably give them each a million dollars when I kiss that freakin' zoo goodbye. But me get up and drive out there at six in the morning five or six days a week anymore? No, no, no, no, no, no, *no!*"

"So then," the reporter said, "are you planning on giving away a large portion of your newly acquired fortune?"

"Oh, sure," Hunny said. "Why not? There'll be plenty to go around. Art and I will probably have some work done on the house..."

"Yeah, like blow it up!" somebody yelled, and this produced more laughter.

"And Art was reminding me just the other day that we need four new tires on the Explorer..."

Now a man who had been part of the kick line was being

nudged forward by other celebrants, and we recognized him from earlier in the report. The reporter said, "And here is somebody else who may have his own ideas about what you can do with your billion dollars. This is Hunny's partner, Arthur Malanowski. Art, please share your feelings with us on this momentous occasion."

A grinning long-faced man with a red nose and thinning straw-colored hair, Malanowski moved tipsily but spoke clearly in a fluty baritone. "Well, dearie, we *are* going to have to talk to an attorney, and I guess to an investment advisor. Right now, though, we're just going to party, party, party!"

"Art is the grown-up of the household," Hunny said cheerfully, waving his champagne glass at his sweetheart and sloshing a bit of its contents onto Art's green, blue, orange and yellow Hawaiian shirt. "But what I have to remind him of is that *neither* of us has to act like a grown-up *ever again!*"

"He's pulling your leg," Malanowski said chortling. "Hunny is basically levelheaded."

Somebody in the room started chanting, "No, he's not!" and others picked it up. "No, he's not! No, he's not…!"

Then they all cheered as Hunny said, "I'm gonna act just as grown-up as America's all-time favorite billionaire, which means wherever I go there's gonna be a Pontiac under everybody's seat from now on!"

Timmy said, "Uh oh."

Suddenly looking a little more sober, Malanowski said, "Hunny is well known for being generous, and I'm sure he will continue that. But in a kind of organized way. Maybe like Paul Newman. A foundation or whatever."

"Artie, luv, you are *my* Paul Newman," Hunny crooned, and planted a big wet kiss on Malanowski's cheek. "And I'm your Bea Arthur!"

"Hunny, Paul Newman wasn't married to Bea Arthur."

"Yes, he was!" Hunny insisted, and another chant broke out all around the room — "Yes, he was! Yes, he was!" — before trailing away into raucous laughter.

The TV reporter asked, "How long have you two been a couple? I get the impression it's been quite some time you've been together."

"Oh, girl!" Hunny sang out, waving his arm and flinging an inch of cigarette ash onto the reporter's blue jacket. "Arthur and I have been lovebirds since before *you* were even born. We're not actually legally married, what with the State of New York still futzing around on the subject of gay marriage. But the reality of the situation is, we are already *so* married — the way we depend on each other and all — that we could give a rat's ass what all those closet queen politicians do or don't do."

"But we would like to make it legal," Malanowski said. "Just to show that we're as good as anybody else."

"And to make sure you're in Hunny's will," somebody yelled, but this produced only scattered guffaws.

"Well," the reporter said gamely, "like a lot of married couples, you two do seem to have quite a bit in common."

"You bet we do," Hunny said. "For example, we both like having buckets of money drop out of nowhere all of a sudden, ha ha ha!"

Malanowski added, "You bet we both like money. After all," he sang, almost in tune, "mon-ey makes the world go 'round... the world go 'round...the world go 'round...""

There were cheers again, and Hunny added, "Money, yes, you bet, but don't forget boys! Boys, boys, boys!"

This led to more applause and then cries of "Bring on the boys! Where are the boys?"

Somebody yelled, "Put the twins on TV! Let's get a little of the twins!"

The large black man reappeared in a voluminous pink satin blouse, and this time he was guiding the two identical youths wearing WANT SOME? T-shirts into the center of the scene. Hunny welcomed them by wrapping his arms around them and bellowing, "Everybody meet Tyler and Schuyler. These are our pool boys! Aren't they *adorable?*"

The two comely lads stood looking goggle-eyed and twitchy, and plainly under the influence of a controlled substance.

The reporter was beginning to look uncomfortable now and glanced off to the side, maybe at her producer. She said to Hunny — and then immediately looked as if she wished she hadn't said it — "But you don't have a swimming pool, do you, Hunny?"

"The boys may have misplaced it. They're easily distracted," Hunny said, and this elicited a mixture of laughter and boos around the room. Tyler and Schuyler gawked into the camera.

"Anyway," Art said, "maybe we'll have a pool put in tomorrow. The Luntzes, up the street, have an aboveground pool, and we know there's room for one of those out back."

"We have to wait until we actually get our hands on the money," Hunny explained. "We've decided on the lump sum of a billion dollars instead of one billion, eight-hundred-seventy-two million spread out over twenty years. I mean, I could croak in three years and so could the freakin' state of New York."

"I understand," the reporter said, "that the Lottery Commission is actually paying out nearly two billion dollars so that even after taxes you will still end up with an entire billion dollars."

"Hey, does Warren Buffet pay his own taxes?" Hunny asked. "Not on your life."

"We're going to get the check on Friday," Art said. "They're going to present it to us on *The Today Show.* Isn't that fabulous? They probably don't remember that about ten years ago when we went down to hold up a sign on Hunny's birthday, he got arrested for mooning Al Roker."

"I wasn't *arrested,*" Hunny insisted. "I was just locked in an office until the show was over. And anyway the security guard — one of the biggest queens I ever saw wearing a uniform — that big black ol' Miss Mary Mary Quite Contrary told me that Al thought it was pretty funny, and the problem was tight-assed

Katie Couric."

Timmy said, "We have to put this on the calendar. Friday morning at seven."

"Maybe we should have a few people over."

The Channel 13 reporter didn't look as eager as Timmy and I were to witness this groundbreaking media event, and also she appeared to be receiving signals from somewhere to wind up the interview.

Before she could speak, though, the screen suddenly went black. A few seconds later one of the anchors on the studio news set appeared and said, "Well, it looks like we've lost Tiffany."

"Yes," said his female colleague, "But wasn't that fascinating?"

Looking unsure of how to respond — even this codger seemed to understand that *hint of mint* cracks were a thing of the past — the anchor simply nodded and moved on to the house fires and convenience store holdups that somebody at the TV station thought the people of New York State's capital region needed to know about.

CHAPTER TWO

"Uncle Hunny asked for trouble, and he got it," Nelson Van Horn said, indicating the man slouched in a chair across from me. "You just cannot live the life my uncle's led and not have chickens coming home to roost by the dozens — by the hundreds, for heaven's sake! And it certainly doesn't help when you go on television and flaunt your irresponsible lifestyle, and at the same time you're practically wearing a sign that says THREATEN ME, BLACKMAIL ME, EXPLOIT ME. Uncle Hunny," Nelson went on, shaking his head with exasperation, "what in God's name did you *expect* was going to happen when you said all those idiotic things about giving away millions of dollars? Especially considering all the incredibly sleazy people you've chosen to associate with over the years?"

Art Malanowski was seated next to Hunny looking much more subdued than he'd been on Channel 13 Wednesday night or on *The Today Show* on Friday. It was Saturday morning now, and the three men were not just tense and unhappy but also wilting in the tropical heat of my Central Avenue office. The air conditioner was on the fritz again, and I had the window above the useless unit propped open with my twenty-year-old bicycle pump, itself no longer operable.

"Nelson, don't you talk to *me* about sleazy!" Hunny shot back. "Girl, you had just better watch your tongue when it comes to sleaze, what with you working for those Wall Street rip-off artists who practically made the whole economy of the country crash down on everybody's head but yourselves. If you calling my friends sleazy isn't the pot calling the kettle un-ironed chiffon, I don't know what is."

"Uncle Hunny, let's have a reality check here. Can we just do that? First of all, Livingston Brothers is one of the most conservative investment concerns in the country, and we have been injured by the current downturn just like every other financial institution. Badly off as we are for the moment, we have few personal regrets down on State Street. Secondly, it is *you* whose past is finally catching up with you. Good grief, why would we even be sitting here talking to a detective if you hadn't been so totally reckless and irresponsible, chasing after all those seedy characters for all those years. And you *still* don't know how to control yourself." Nelson looked at me and said, "Did you catch Uncle Hunny on *The Today Show* yesterday?"

I said I had.

"Well, you tell me, Don. Did Uncle Hunny do himself any good — or the cause of gay rights or gay marriage any good — by complimenting Matt Lauer on his 'nice basket'?"

Hunny and Art looked at each other, grinned and gave each other a fist bump. "For goodness' sakes, I thought we were already off the air," Hunny said, and then he and Art started giggling all over again.

The nephew, a carefully toned, attentively groomed man in his early forties, sighed heavily and said to me, "So you can see what we're up against."

I said, "Matt Lauer seemed to take the comment in stride. It isn't clear he even knew what your uncle meant."

"Oh, girl, he *knew*," Hunny piped up.

Art added, "Don't you believe, dearie, that that was the first time anybody ever said something nice about his bulge to Missy Matt Lauer. And everybody knows about the casting couch at NBC. Do you think those people on those shows get those jobs just on their looks?"

"Brian Williams, Alex Trebek, Chris Matthews, Perry Como back in the old days — they all had to put out," Hunny said and mimed an act of fellatio.

"Do you see what I mean?" Nelson said to me disgustedly. "Is it any wonder that somebody on Moth Street cut the Channel 13 cable the other night with an ax, presumably to shut my out-of-control uncle up?"

"Nelson," Hunny said, "them thar was outside agitators that chopped up the TV line. None of Arty's and my neighbors feel that way about us or would do such a thing on the night of my lifetime achievement award. Well, maybe the Brownlees. Or the Haneses. Or Peter Petengill. They all hate our guts. Or Evelyn Seltzer."

"Possibly the Fromes," Art mused additionally.

"Now you are making my point for me," Nelson said to his uncle. "Some people just do not appreciate your flamboyant personalities and have it in for you. They don't like the constant sexual innuendos, and they don't at all like the activities that everybody thinks go on behind those innuendos."

"It is true," Hunny said, "that some people think it's tacky pulling college boys' underpants down as often as possible and enjoying a nice gobble. But certainly *you* are not one of those narrow-minded people, Nelson."

"Ho!" Nelson rolled his eyes. "If *only* they were college boys."

I said, "So, are you also gay, Nelson?"

"Yes, I am. There seems to be one of those genes jumping around in the Van Horn family. But it's one thing to be gay and it's another thing entirely to make a sorry, obscene spectacle of yourself, and your family, and most of gay America. A friend who works for the Human Rights Campaign in Washington called me last night and asked if there wasn't anything I could do to control Uncle Hunny. This man, who my partner went to Dartmouth with, saw *The Today Show* fiasco, and he pointed out — as if I needed reminding — that Art and Uncle Hunny were playing right into the religious right's hands."

Hunny said, "Nelson's boyfriend is so drop-dead *fab*-ulous that hardly anybody can stand it. He's into derivatives, which have gone out of fashion, though he is just too, *too* fashionable otherwise. The two of them have places — *places* is what they call them — in Clifton Park and Palm Springs. Nelson's squeeze is named Lawn Brookman, spelled L-A-W-N. Art and I call him Yawn."

"So, Nelson," I said, "it's not only your uncle's well-being that led you to bring him to me? Are you also hoping I might help alter his personality? That's really outside my area of expertise."

Nelson slumped wearily. "The reason I am involving myself in this ridiculous business at all is to protect Uncle Hunny from his own worst instincts and from the people his bad instincts have gotten him involved with. I admit I have no real hope that Uncle Hunny will change. Just acting a little more discreet in public is what I'm hoping for. For his sake, and for our family's sake, especially my parents — but also Grandma Rita, Uncle Hunny's poor mother."

Hunny glared. "Nelson, anything I do or say is just fine with Mom. Always has been, always will be." To me, Hunny said, "My sister Miriam, Nelson's mother, is just a sad lost cause sexual-orientation-wise. Miriam thinks PFLAG is an insect repellent. And my brother-in-law Lewis tells his golfing buddies that Nelson isn't married because his fiancé died on 9/11 in the World Trade Center, and he is still too broken up over it to start dating again."

"Not true," Nelson said, looking even more despondent. "My parents are conservative, but they are not bigots and they are not mean-spirited. They simply observe certain standards of taste, about which Uncle Hunny plainly knows nothing. I don't understand that, really. Grandma Rita has had her personal difficulties, and now her mind is not what it once was. But she has always been well-mannered in her outgoing way, and I know she is well-respected out at Golden Gardens. And Grandpa Carl also set high behavioral standards. He was a well-spoken, churchgoing man who always went out of his way to make other people feel comfortable. Uncle Hunny, on the other hand, seems to take great pleasure in making people feel *un*comfortable."

"I have standards of taste, too," Hunny said, winking at Art. "Except, I have certain standards of *bad* taste I try to live by. To each his own, Nelson, to each his own."

Art said, "Nelson, your father did so tell people you had a girlfriend who was killed on 9/11. That came back to Hunny and me from several sources. She was supposedly a securities analyst, and her name was Gwen Bainbridge, Lewis told people."

"Miriam and Lewis," Hunny said, "talk about Lawn as Nelson's roommate. Like they're twenty years old and live in a dorm."

"Hunny, according to some of these blackmail attempts," I said, indicating the bundle of computer printouts the three men had brought along with them to my office, "a number of the things people are saying about you go beyond questions of taste. Lowbrow high-spiritedness is one thing, but some of these people say they have proof that you've done things that are illegal. For instance, serving alcohol to minors. The law takes that seriously, as I'm sure you know. And you've had phone calls now from — how many? seven? — young men who say you got them drunk and had sex with them. Are any of these guys telling the truth?"

Hunny snatched a pack of Marlboros out of his shirt pocket and lit one with a butane lighter. "Now, lookie here, girl," he said, shooting smoke and spittle my way, "I am not now and never have been into serious chicken. A boy has to be old enough to know better, or I'm not interested. Well, interested maybe. I'm only human. But I don't ever mess around with some youngster's emotions. It's fun I want, and I want a boy who's old enough to know what he wants, especially if what he wants is just to have some fun. It's true that sometimes a twenty-one-year-old needs a little lubrication to loosen up his inhibitions, just like I did when I was twenty-one and just like Nelson did." Hunny's nephew stiffened and, if I wasn't mistaken, blushed. "It's possible, of course," Hunny went on, "that a few of these boys might have been just a smidgen short of twenty-one. I mean, if a kid is obviously post-adolescent I don't see any need to check his driver's license. Would you?"

Hunny seemed to be addressing me. I said, "I'm in a long-time relationship, but that's beside the point. I don't have young guys from my past lining up and threatening to haul me into court unless I cough up thousands of dollars. You do. Can any of these under-twenty-ones prove that you got them sauced up and then — did whatever it is you do?"

"Gave them blowjobs," Hunny said cheerfully, glancing around for an ashtray and then flicking ash into my wastebasket. "There could be a few pictures out there somewhere. No videos, though, I don't think. And no pictures from any of the guys who have called so far."

Nelson muttered bitterly, "Oh, so far. That's great."

Art said, "Hunny, if anybody accused you of being a pedophile, you could get testimony from tons of people saying you like sex with guys of all ages."

"Like at work," Hunny said. "I've blown half the straight guys at the warehouse. But they're mostly married, so I really can't say how many of them would stand up for me. Hey," Hunny added. "Good choice of words — stand up for me," and he and Art cackled.

Nelson looked close to tears.

"And then in addition to the men who are explicitly threatening to expose you for illegal acts," I said, "are a dozen or so who have asked for money and used language where there's an implicit threat. We're talking nearly twenty of these characters to deal with, and maybe more on the way, no? If I do take you on as a client, Hunny, this could run into time and money. As a sexually active gay man about town, you've had a busy career. Tracking all these guys down and then explaining to them in the nicest way possible that blackmail and extortion are illegal in the state of New York could take up a sizeable chunk of my work week or month." I went over my standard fee schedule, and as I sat across from not-so-plutocrat-looking Hunny and Art, I left off the surcharge I normally add for any billionaires who find their way to my Central Avenue walkup.

Hunny looked at me speculatively and said, "Your office is kind of tacky, but your rates aren't."

"Those are my normal fees. Once in a while people ask for their money back, but most are satisfied."

Hunny smiled and said, "Don, have you ever fooled around

with an older, more experienced man?"

"I *told* you, Uncle Hunny, that Donald is gay. That's one reason I brought you to him. But he just told you that he has a boyfriend. God, can't you *ever* leave it alone? All this sex, sex, sex, sex. People just get *sick* of it."

Hunny flapped his wrist at his nephew. "Well, get *her*!" He looked over at me and said, "Nelson and Yawn prefer collecting gym equipment to collecting boys. How silly can a drag queen be?"

"Do you and your partner do drag?" I asked Nelson conversationally and maybe because I was curious as to what I might get Hunny to come out with next.

Nelson said, "Lawn and I do not do drag, no. That's just the way my uncle talks. Constantly."

"When you were twelve," Art said, "you got caught wearing your mother's underwear. Hunny's mom told us about that."

Art and Hunny chuckled, and Nelson went red again. "Uncle Hunny, I am *trying* to be helpful. You called me and asked me if I knew anybody who could deal with these ghastly seedy characters who came oozing out of the woodwork as soon as you won the lottery. I bring you to this man who knows how to deal with predatory scumbags and might be able to keep you from being conned, or even — let's just get it right out there — out of jail. And what do you do? You and Art spend the entire time insulting me and dishing detective Strachey. So, do you want help, or do you not? If you do, then I suggest that you start acting like a mature adult for the first time in your life."

"Anyway," Hunny said, "I've been in jail before. That's something I know I can handle, if it comes to that."

"That was entirely different," Nelson said. "This time it wouldn't be about social protest. It would be about corrupting a minor or something really serious you couldn't wriggle out of so easily. And it wouldn't just be overnight, either."

I asked, "You were arrested at a protest, Hunny?"

"Yes, on June twenty-eighth, 1969." He smiled at me and batted his eyelashes and flapped his wrist once.

"Stonewall? You were there?" I had goose bumps.

"Both of us were," Art said. "Hunny and I met when they shoved us both in the same paddy wagon."

"Wow."

"Some of us in the Van Horn family," Nelson said, "are actually quite proud of Art and Uncle Hunny. Lawn and I are both grateful for the social revolution that made it possible for us to live as comfortably and openly as we do as gay men. But that was then and this is now, and throwing beer bottles at the police is no longer either appropriate or necessary. And there certainly is no need anymore for gay men to go around shrieking defiantly and sexualizing every utterance and affecting the personalities of ten-year-old girls. Art and Hunny and the other people at Stonewall that night could afford to act like that because they had nothing to lose. But now, thanks to the post-Stonewall social gains, we all have plenty to lose. And lose things we most certainly will if our most prominent role models go on TV and start rolling their eyes and waving their arms around and shrieking about Matt Lauer's 'nice basket.'"

As Nelson gave his speech, Hunny made a show of looking bored, and then he picked up the lists of blackmailers and extortionists that he had placed on my desk earlier.

Paying no attention to anything Nelson had said, Hunny looked up at me with a queasy expression. "You know, Don," he said, "there are a couple of these humpy numbers that we might have to end up paying something to. Annoying as that would be."

"Why is that?" I said.

"Because two or three of them I think would have to be considered maybe kind of…dangerous?"

Art leaned over and peered at the list and nodded, and Nelson slid even farther down in his chair.

CHAPTER THREE

"I think I should get half," Stu Hood said. "It's only fair. Hunny told me lots of times he was gonna ditch Art and marry me. Just 'cause Hunny never got around to doing what he promised is no reason for me to suffer. Anyway, I was underage when Hunny popped my cherry. That's against the law, and I was an impressionable youth."

"How old were you?" I asked.

"When Hunny introduced me to the homosexual lifestyle, I was eighteen or nineteen years of age, I forget which. I was only a child."

"But the age of consent in New York is seventeen, Stu. Dewy-browed stripling that you might have considered yourself to be, in the eyes of the law you were a consenting adult."

"No shit. I thought you had to be twenty-one."

"To drink, yes. But not for sex. Voting is eighteen and alcohol consumption twenty-one, but seventeen is the age of consent for sex in New York."

"Well, he served me alcohol."

"Uh huh."

"He told me it was happy hour on Moth Street."

"This was in Hunny's house?"

"Yeah, Art wasn't home and Hunny was sneaking a quickie, apparently."

We were seated at a table near the dimly lit rear of the Watering Hole, a gay bar of robust semi-down-at-the-heels antiquity down the street from my office on Central Avenue. Hunny had told me an hour earlier that Hood was likely to be hanging out there on a Saturday, and Hunny had been right. The bartender had pointed Hood out, a hatchet-faced, late twenty-something, stringily muscular man in cargo pants and a tank top, with afternoon beer on his breath.

I asked, "Had you been acquainted with Hunny previous to your accompanying him to his house?"

"Yeah, I'd talked to him a few times in the park. But only talk. I was cherry."

"Washington Park?"

"Sure."

"Are you a naturalist, or did you hang out in the park trying to get picked up?"

"I was bi-curious, yeah. But I never did much of anything with guys till Hunny lured me into his car and took me over to his place and committed a lewd act. So, Hunny owes me. Hunny owes me *big*."

"You said, Stu, that you believe Hunny should give you half of his lottery winnings. Do you honestly believe Hunny owes you half a billion dollars for a blow job? That sounds steep to me. These days I'm guessing you only get twenty or thirty bucks."

"Sometimes fifty," Hood said. "Anyways, with Hunny I just did it for the beer. He was nice to me, and I was nice to him back."

"So you and Hunny had a continuing relationship after your initial visit?"

"Yeah, I'd ride my bike over there, and sometimes Art would show up and get a little, too. I'm not saying they weren't nice to me. All I'm saying at this point in time is that Hunny did turn me into a homosexual, and then he did make certain promises. Like maybe I could move in sometime and be part of their alternative family. That would have suited me fine."

The bar was surprisingly busy for a summer afternoon. The air-conditioning probably served as an attraction, and in any case the two dozen or so patrons did not look like either beachgoers or men who might otherwise have been off on Adirondack birding expeditions. Some of the men in the bar glanced our way from time to time, maybe wondering who Hood's new friend was.

I said, "Stu, you're a cyclist. How come?"

I knew what was coming. "I lost my driver's license. Too many DUIs. It sucks, but I'm sort of used to it. It's rough in the winter, though. People give me rides."

"Have you had any other legal troubles?"

"A few."

"Hunny says you like to set fires."

Hood looked down at his draught beer. Almost inaudibly, he said, "I guess so."

"He said you had an arson conviction as a juvenile."

"Yes, I did. But I've been to counseling."

"You left a message on Hunny's voicemail threatening to burn his house down if he didn't split his lottery winnings with you."

He shrugged. "That was bullshit. I was drunk up to my eyeballs when I said that. Shit, Hunny should know."

"I'm here to tell you, Stu, that if Hunny and Art's house goes up in flames, you will be arrested in a short time. And if you set the fire, you will be convicted and you will go to prison for a very long time. Do you understand what I am telling you?"

Hood mulled this over and had some more beer. "I guess Hunny must be pissed at me."

"He is concerned about you. Hunny likes you, and he doesn't want to see you locked up in Dannemora for twenty years. He said to tell you also that he would be willing to help you out financially, some small amount to tide you over. But half a billion is out."

"Hunny is so cheap. How much did he say?"

"He said he heard you had been laid off at Target, and he said he would be happy to spring for a thousand to help you along until you located another job."

"Hmm. Check or cash?"

"Whichever you would prefer."

"Cash money, please."

"But no more threats, okay?"

"Well, shit, it's more than I got out of the Catholic Church."

"You sued the church?"

"I wrote a letter to the pope. He never answered it. A priest at Sacred Heart fucked me seven times when I was eleven."

"But there were lawsuits over sexual abuse by priests, and victims were compensated. This was several years ago."

"I heard about that later."

The music playing now was Donna Summer's "On the Radio." It occurred to me that the first time I had heard this song could well have been in this very bar some decades earlier, perhaps on the same night I met Timothy Callahan under a bush over in Washington Park, and we had been together pretty much ever since. I raised my bottle of Saratoga Water with a chunk of lime jammed down into it. *To Donna Summer.*

To Hood, I said, "The church did shut down the compensation machinery at some point. Didn't your friends urge you to file a claim before it was too late? Did Hunny know about this?"

"I didn't tell anybody back then. In fact, I kind of forgot about it. A guy I was involved with for a while kept asking me why I didn't like to get fucked, and then I remembered."

"And that's when you wrote to the pope?"

"Another guy I used to date who had a computer helped me send an e-mail to the Vatican. Maybe the pope only speaks Italian, but there must be other dudes who work in his office who speak English. I think the guy is just a geek, that's all."

"You said you've had counseling. When was that?"

"At the farm the judge sent me to. I was thirteen years of age. Anyway, that wasn't about sex, it was about fires."

"Have you had any problems with the law since then? Hunny said he was unaware of any run-ins. But he said that when you drink you sometimes threaten to set people's houses on fire, or their cars, and it is very frightening to people."

"That's just the Bud Lite talking," Hood said. "I would never do it. Hunny doesn't have to worry. Though I would appreciate a little compensation for Hunny turning me into a homo, since it looks like the friggin' pope is gonna be of no use to me whatsoever."

"Hunny told me about your parents," I said. "And about the terrible way they died. That must weigh on you, too."

"Hunny has a big mouth."

"It's why even though he is fond of you, he is somewhat afraid of you."

"Yeah, well. Mom and Pop never replaced the battery in their smoke alarm. Does he know that part of it? Let that be a lesson to Hunny."

"Stu, what you are saying to me isn't all that reassuring."

"What I'm saying to you, Strachey, is that I don't set fires anymore. I'm all talk. Talk and beer, beer and talk. And if it's reassurance you want on a Saturday afternoon, this homo bar is not the place to find it."

CHAPTER FOUR

Hunny was back on the Channel 13 news Saturday evening at six. This time he was defending his lottery boodle not against blackmailers but against a co-worker at BJ's Warehouse who claimed that half of Hunny's winnings were rightfully his. Dave DeCarlo said he had given Hunny ten dollars to buy twenty dollars' worth of tickets for the two of them, and they had agreed to split the winnings from any of the tickets purchased.

DeCarlo, who was interviewed first, along with his attorney, Thurmont Fewster, said it was the deep pain of being betrayed by a man he had always thought of as a friend that was hurting him most of all. His lawyer focused on what he referred to as a "broken oral contract."

When it was Hunny's turn, he said that while he and DeCarlo had once purchased lottery tickets together, that had been back in the spring and had been for an entirely different drawing, not the August Instant Warren. Hunny added that while he had planned on giving all his co-workers what he called an "August bonus" from his lottery winnings, now that DeCarlo was trying to swindle him, "that *bleep bleep*" wasn't going to get a cent.

Timmy and I were watching the news in our bedroom at our house on Crow Street before heading out for a Saturday night Thai dinner with friends. After that, I planned on meeting another of the blackmailers when his cleaning-crew shift at a Corporate Woods office building ended at eleven.

Timmy said, "Hunny is quite the sleazoid-magnet. It looks as if he's going to keep you hopping."

"DeCarlo does appear to be an unscrupulous fellow. Most of the other skeletons tumbling out of Hunny's voluminous closet, though, look like they're just hapless shmoes. I phoned three of them this morning after Hunny left my office and warned them off, and none of the ones I talked to seemed to want any trouble. I'm more worried about two other guys who do sound a bit unhinged and maybe even dangerous. I saw one of them this afternoon at the Watering Hole. He's a hustler named Stu Hood who has a history of arson."

"Oh no."

"He has only one conviction, as a juvenile, but Hunny says the guy was a suspect in a number of later cases. When Hood was thirteen, he burned down his parents' house with them in it. He was supposed to be out mowing the lawn, but instead he poured gasoline from the lawn mower can all around the downstairs and lit it and ran out. He told the police he didn't know his mother and father were upstairs napping and that he thought they had gone out for the afternoon. But Hunny said the family car was in the driveway, so Hood's story was widely doubted. On Thursday, Hood threatened Hunny and told him he would torch his and Art's house if Hunny didn't go fifty-fifty with Hood on the lottery winnings. He claims Hunny turned him into a homosexual after Hunny picked him up while Hood was cruising the park."

"Why, Donald, it's *our* story."

"Exactly. I was a confused youth, and when you fondled me behind that bush, I thought, oh, wow, I could get used to this."

"You were the mixed-up youth? I'm reasonably certain it was the other way around."

"Then how come you were carrying that towel thing around with you at eleven o'clock at night? You even told me at the time that it was so you wouldn't get moss on your knees."

"I seem to have repressed any memory of that."

"Anyway, Hood's story is as ugly as it gets. He told me that he was repeatedly raped by a priest when he was eleven years old but that he didn't recall these incidents until it was too late for any legal recourse."

"Do you believe him?"

"I'm not sure. But it was two years later that he started setting fires. Or two years that anybody knows of."

"Were there any church fires around that time?"

"Good question. But my role here is not to prosecute or to clear Stu Hood for any crimes he may have committed in years gone by. My job is to get him off Hunny Van Horn's back."

Timmy zapped off the TV — no more Hunny news for the moment — and started getting into his dinner togs, his nicely pressed slacks and a polo shirt he had ironed earlier in the day. He said, "I keep hearing that gay people in the Capitol really do wish somebody other than Hunny had won the Instant Warren. He is just such an excruciating public embarrassment."

"I find him interesting and sometimes even entertaining," I said. "Hunny is one of a vanishing species. Also, here is a client who, when I bill him at the end of the month, will be in a good position to pay it."

"Vanishing species, I don't think so. God, if only."

"Hunny is gay man at his most primitive. He's the untamed queer Neanderthal. He's the rugged individualist on the old gay frontier. He's a homo Huck before Aunt Polly tried to civilize him. Hunny is proudly out and proudly nelly. Hunny am what he am."

"What Hunny am," Timmy said, "is a loudmouth drunk and a hideous old letch. It wouldn't surprise me if the greatest threat to Hunny at this point is not some juvenile delinquent arsonist he had sex with, but any of the thousands of decent, sober, well-behaved gay men and women across America who see Hunny on national television and are now looking for ways to make this grotesquely embarrassing creature just disappear."

Timmy had at least a partial point. Maybe looking after Hunny was going to be even more complicated than I thought.

∫ ∫ ∫ ∫

The first thing Mason Doebler said to me was, "I'm not taking any shit from Hunny and I'm not taking any shit from you. Don't waste your time threatening me, and don't waste your time pissing me off. Hunny has owed me three thousand dollars for four years, and now he can afford to pay his debt to me — with interest."

"He told me that the other day you demanded fifty thousand dollars. That represents a lot of interest on three K. It's even more than Citibank charges."

"I'm charging him a lot because now that he's won the lottery, fifty K means nothing to Hunny. And because his refusal to pay me anything at all has been a thorn in my side that I am sick of. I have it coming, and, believe me, I am going to get it."

Doebler looked like a man who, when he made demands, generally had them met. A good six-three, two-forty, with a crew cut above a whiskery moon face, he had the heft and sartorial coloration of a gay bear but not one with a cuddly demeanor. We were seated at a table in the upstairs restaurant in a noisy bar on Lark Street. The music was some type of heavy metal lite, though the band playing it did not appear on any of the eight large flat TV screens arrayed around the room. These were showing a variety of sporting events — baseball, pre-season football, NASCAR — and the overall feel of the place was that of a rest home for people with severe ADD.

Doebler was chowing down on two double chili burgers, and I was keeping my grip moist on a sweating bottle of Sam Adams.

I said, "Hunny told me that you think he was responsible for wrecking your car. But he says none of what happened four years ago was his fault, and he accepts no financial responsibility. What's your side of the story, Mason?"

Through a mouthful of dough and ground beef, Doebler said, "Hunny was sucking my dick while I was driving out Western Avenue near SUNY, and I ran off the road and smashed into some bushes. The air bags went off, and we didn't get hurt much. But my Firebird was a mess and my collision insurance had a three thousand dollar deductible. I had *told* Hunny to wait till we got to his place. But Hunny'd had a few cocktails — as Hunny always does — and he was totally out of control, as usual. He was smoking a cigarette, too, and we were just lucky we didn't go up in flames. Getting the Firebird back on the road cost over five thousand, and three thousand of that was out of pocket. *My* pocket, even though Hunny was totally to blame."

"Something doesn't quite add up here, Mason. Are you claiming that while you were driving your car, Hunny raped you?"

"Of course not."

"But you are saying, as I understand it, that your erect penis was out in the open air, and Hunny was bent over and sucking it. Did you take your dick out of your pants, or did Hunny?"

"Well, he did. That's what I'm *saying*."

"It must have taken Hunny some minutes to get your pants open or down around your ankles. During that time, why did you not pull to the side of the road — taking proper care and utilizing your directional signals — and retrieve your dick from Hunny and place it back in your trousers where you claim you wanted it to remain?"

Doebler glared at me and said, "You know goddam well why I didn't make him stop. If somebody is sucking your cock — and they're as good as Hunny is at it — you're not really thinking clearly. But I did *tell* Hunny to fucking cut it out."

"If we were in a court of law, I doubt you could fall back on ambivalence as a justification for your behavior. Or temporary insanity, either."

"Look, if Hunny had not been stinko and out of his mind, the whole thing would never have happened. *That's* the point, and that is why Hunny owes me three thousand dollars. No, *fifty*."

I said, "Hunny says that when you called him on Thursday, you threatened him. He has this on his voicemail."

A rivulet of chili sauce ran down Doebler's chin, and he wiped it off with a napkin. "Oh, Hunny told you that, huh?"

"Yes."

"Well, fuck, I was just making a point. And I guess I made it. What with you all of a sudden ragging my ass."

"I understand, Mason, that you have a couple of assault convictions on your record."

"So?"

"This has Hunny concerned. If you choose to sue him for three K, that's your right. But you have no right to hurt him, and I am strongly advising you not to do it."

Doebler, who was having a Coke with his burgers, said, "Those incidents were when I was drinking. I'm sober now, and this enables me to manage my anger. What I said to Hunny the other day was just to get his attention. What's fifty thousand dollars to Hunny, anyway? Why doesn't Hunny just fucking help me out? He could do it with no sweat. I have issues, and he knows it. The suspension on my Firebird is practically shot and the catalytic converter is shit, and the check-engine light is on, and I know that in October I'm not gonna pass inspection. Fuck, it's no skin off Hunny's nose if he helps me out in my time of need. Ah, shit."

I said, "Hunny is willing to give you a thousand. Not as a settlement but as a gift. He said you two had some nice times together, and he is sorry that there are hard feelings. This present, if you took it, would not indicate that he accepts any financial responsibility for the accident. Hunny is sorry it happened, but he believes that it was your own inebriation at the time that was the main cause of your driving off the road. You were still drinking then, Hunny told me."

Doebler shook his head. "Fuck."

"The thousand should cover the catalytic converter and get you an oil change, too."

"I saw Hunny and Art on TV the other night," Doebler said. "That looked like quite a party they were having."

"If you quit pestering Hunny about the three thousand, my guess is he would be willing to let bygones be bygones and you two could be friends again."

Doebler had finished off the first chili burger and now he started in on the second. "Well, I could use the thou. I can't deny that."

"It's up to you, Mason."

Before Doebler could reply, my cell phone went off. I excused myself and walked back toward the men's room, partly for the privacy but also so I could hear anything over the barroom din.

Hunny said, "Donald, girl, I'm *sooo* sorry to be phoning you at this late hour. You're such a good boy and it's probably past your bedtime. But Lawn just called me, and he is extremely upset. He says Nelson has gone off somewhere to deal with a situation I am supposedly the cause of, and he said Nelson told him that I have really done it this time, and Lawn is coming over here to wring my neck."

CHAPTER FIVE

An Albany police cruiser was just pulling away from Hunny and Art's brightly lighted house as I drove up, and I wondered if Hunny's new "situation" had already escalated into a law-enforcement matter. It hadn't, I soon learned, from a group of men ambling down the front steps. They informed me that the cops had come by in response to noise complaints from neighbors. The officers had asked Hunny nicely — he was a celebrity now — to have some consideration. He had graciously agreed, and now the party was winding down and people were heading off to the bars and clubs. A soft-spoken young Hispanic man with enough metal rings in his lower lip to hang a shower curtain on pointed out that there was still plenty of liquor and drugs available inside, and he suggested that I go on inside and help myself to some of "Hunny's good shit."

Hunny's living room looked like the debris field after an air disaster, with dazed survivors lying around on couches and easy chairs while they snacked on Doritos and chips and Price Chopper clam dip. The twins, clad only in red thongs, were very much a presence, one of them doing some perfunctory tidying up, the other chatting idly as he sat on the lap of a man who looked like Karl Rove but probably wasn't. A man in a pink ball gown introduced himself as Marylou Whitney and told me that Hunny and Art were in the kitchen.

"Oh, Donald, you have come to my rescue!" Hunny crooned, as he hung up the wall phone. "I hope you're armed, 'cause Lawn just called again and he is on his way over here to kill me. Nelson is on his way, too, and I think you should shoot them both as soon as they walk in the front door. It's Bette Davis in *The Letter*. *Blam, blam, blam, blam!* You can plead self-defense, and Artie and I will back you up. So, Donnie, *are* you carrying a pistol, or are you just glad to see me?"

"Neither, really. What's going on now, Hunny?"

Hunny was seated at the kitchen table with a glass of something amber in one hand and a cigarette in the other. Art was bent over the sink rinsing out some glasses.

Art said, "We have apparently interfered with Nelson and Lawn's dinner at Jack's Oyster House with some local felons. Dinner at Jack's is a sacred ritual and I guess we have somehow blasphemed. Nelson went off to see some people about Hunny and his money, and he didn't show up for dinner, and now Lawn is all higglety-pigglety-pooglety-swooglety."

Hunny flung some cigarette ash my way. "Nelson supposedly is going to explain it when he gets here, but Lawn said Nelson said some people have demanded half of my billion dollars and we might have to give it to them. I mean, what's half a billion to me, but I have to say, this does sound nervous-making, wouldn't you say?"

"Yeah. It does."

"Now, Donald, girl, I don't like the looks of your dour expression. I think you might need a drink. Are you a Cutty Sark drinker with a Dos Equis chaser? Or how about some weed? What can I get for you, sweetie? What about some dick? The twins are hung like Jeff Stryker, plus they're more interesting. Donald, take a load off and let us entertain you. It bothers me that you're not having any fun. What can we do to cheer you up? You look morose."

"I'm all set, thanks."

Art said, "Nelson and Yawn hang out with these horrible people — the city and county officials and state senators the banks and insurance companies are all paying off to get city and county business. You go into Jack's Oyster house and it looks like a scene from Warner Brothers in 1932. You expect to see Edward G. Robinson at a front table cuddling with his moll and his tommy gun."

"Though it's a miracle those crooks will even be seen at Jack's or anywhere else in public with Lawn nowadays," Hunny said. "Everybody who invested money with Lawn is flat-ass broke.

Lawn specialized in tranches. Derivatives and tranches. Donald, do you know what a tranche is?"

Art said, "It sounds like one of Sarah Palin's kids."

"Nobody knows what a tranche is," Hunny said, "because it's just a bunch of dumb, worthless pieces of paper. Yawn made millions on this phony-baloney crapola and then he got out, and then everybody else went straight down the toilet."

Art waved a sponge at me and said, "Now Lawn is all mopey because the SEC is breathing down everybody's neck and he can't commit highway robbery and get away with it anymore. The poor dear has been forced to operate on a somewhat reduced level of criminal behavior, like income tax evasion or shoplifting."

"Poor, tragic Lawn. We call him Tranche DuBois."

Art hung a freshly washed shot glass on a fork protruding from the drying rack and said, "All these Albany mucky-mucks he no doubt swindled just like he did everybody else put up with Lawn because I'm sure he's sucking their dicks. They're all married closet queens, that crowd."

Hunny picked up on this theme. "It's just like the '70s. You'd go into the back room at the Mineshaft, and all the pols would be there crawling around naked on their hands and knees. Today it's no different — Cuomo, Schumer, the Supreme Court. They're all taking it up the butt and they're all just such disgusting phonies." The shot glass fell off the drying rack and back into the sink, and Hunny said, "Artie, dear, why don't you come set for a spell and have another mai tai? At least until Nelson gets here, I'll be the darky and you be the lady."

"Oh, pshaw," Art said, waving Hunny down into his seat, where he poured more of what appeared to be whiskey from a plastic pitcher with a spout shaped like a daisy.

I said, "Did Lawn give you any idea who might be in a position to insist on being paid half a billion dollars?"

"No," Hunny said. "Stu Hood wanted half a billion, but he's only getting a thou, and that sorry little fire setter will have to be grateful for that."

"He's an arsonist," Art said, "but, Lord, is that boy hung."

Now there was some commotion in the other room, and soon a tall, austere-looking man wearing an Armani jacket and ten thousand dollars' worth of pectorals strode into the room.

"Congratulations, Hunny," the man said, not smiling, "for doing the absolutely most idiotic thing you have done so far. You are going to hear all about it when Nelson gets here. He left Cobleskill forty-five minutes ago, and he is on his way here, and Nelson is so upset I had to talk him down and tell him to pull off the road if he felt he couldn't drive safely." Taking note of me, he said, "Are you the private investigator? I'm Lawn Brookman."

"Don Strachey."

"I am Nelson's partner. He said you seemed to be on top of things, which I was quite relieved to hear, and that I could go ahead and brief you."

"Yes, I'd like to hear about this one."

"Nelson used to faint," Hunny said. "When he was thirteen, he passed out in church and had to be carried out. It was a salt deficiency or something."

Art said, "Lawn, did you tell Nelson to put his head down between his legs?"

Hunny laughed and said, "Ooo, *that* should help. For those who can do it."

"The twins almost can," Art said, rinsing out an olive jar.

"And we have that one video," Hunny added.

Lawn glared at Hunny. "Do you two *ever* think about anything besides sexual activity? When Nelson arrives you'll have a whole new topic of conversation, I can guarantee you that."

Hunny lit another cigarette from one that was smoked down to the filter and about to go out. "If you say so, Aunt Eller."

"You know, it was tremendously awkward, Hunny, meeting people for dinner and Nelson not showing up without calling. He was so upset and distracted that he neglected to phone or text and inform me he would be unable to meet us. And when I was unable to explain his absence I was both concerned and irritated, and I'm sure people noticed. They probably thought it was something *I* did or said. It was incredibly embarrassing. Then when Nelson phoned midway through the meal, he said I should not actually tell people where he was and what he was involved with, and I had to make something up. Instead of saying it was about Hunny's mother, I said he was dealing with a cousin who had been in a boating accident. But now my dinner companions will look in the paper about a boating accident, and there won't be any, and I will look like such a fool."

Hunny looked up. "This has something to do with Mom?"

"With some people she used to work for," Lawn said. "He didn't say what it was, just that it was serious and it might involve a large part of Hunny's lottery winnings. Half of the winnings, in fact."

Art put down his sponge and turned to face us, and Hunny lit a second cigarette. One was now smoldering in his filthy ashtray and the second he held in a hand that was trembling slightly.

Hunny said, "Were these people the Brienings?"

"Nelson didn't mention their names."

I asked, "Who are the Brienings?"

"They own a crafts store out in Cobleskill," Art said. "It's where Rita worked until she retired thirteen years ago."

"Is there any reason," I asked, "that the Brienings might think they can extort half a billion dollars from you, Hunny?"

After a moment he mumbled, "Maybe."

Art said, "Lawn, don't you know who the Brienings are?"

"No, I never heard the name before."

"How long have you and Nelson been together?" I asked.

"Eleven years. We met when I came back to Albany after establishing myself in the city in the financial world, and I felt ready to return to my roots and make a name for myself."

"Mary," Art said.

"Nelson and I met in the locker room of our gym on my third day back in Albany, and we have rarely spent a day apart since then. We are just wonderfully well suited for one another, and I consider myself just incredibly lucky to have found my perfect match."

Art had dried his hands on a paper towel, and now he went over and sat next to Hunny, who was starting to look queasy.

Hunny said, "Lawn, please shut the door, will you, dear?"

"This one is definitely not for the laundry basket," Art said.

Lawn closed the door to the living room and said, "What laundry basket?"

"The laundry basket where we put all the letters and messages that have been coming in since Wednesday asking for money or trying to blackmail me," Hunny said. "The basket is down in the basement, and it's overflowing with piles and piles of all kinds of stuff. Mostly it's people who want me to invest in something, or who want a donation for a walk or a swim for some awful disease, or their house was in a flood in Georgia or something. One lady said her astrologer told her I was her first husband in Australia and I still owe her child support. Most of the letters and phone messages are harmless like that, but some are mean and creepy and threatening. The nasty ones are the ones Donald is handling. If this is the Brienings, Nelson has been in touch with, Donald — girl, this is definitely a job for you."

"The Brienings are evil," Art said. "I hope you're ready to wrestle with Satan's spawn, Donald."

"Who are these people?" Lawn said. "I've never even heard their name before. And Grandma Rita worked for them?"

Hunny moaned. "Maybe I should just write them a check and that will be the end of it. Maybe I should look at this as an opportunity not to be missed, and maybe finally they'll just go away."

"How would you go about making out a check for half a

billion dollars?" Art said. "Would you write on it five hundred million, or half a billion, or what? And would there be room to write in all those zeros in that tiny space they give you to write out the numbers?"

Lawn stared. "You've got a billion dollars in your checking account, Hunny?"

"Did you think I was going to stuff it down my cleavage? It's actually one billion, four hundred and fifty-seven dollars. I checked the ATM on the way home this afternoon."

"That giant check they gave Hunny on *The Today Show*," Art said, "was a fake, just for show. The lottery commission provides you with direct deposit if you want it. Which is great. Direct deposit — that's how I get my state pension and my Social Security. In Hunny's case, it was a really good idea, so that on the way back from the city Hunny wouldn't lose the check while he was blowing a truck driver at a Thruway service area."

Hunny chuckled and said, "There's an excellent reason they call them 'service areas,'" and Art snickered, too.

On cue, Lawn looked aghast, and he didn't look any happier when the kitchen door opened and one of the twins strolled in in his thong carrying more dirty glasses on a tray.

"Tyler, dearest, just leave everything till tomorrow morning," Art said.

"Yes," Hunny added. "You and Schuyler should go on out and enjoy yourselves. Artie and I are not going to make it to Rocks tonight, it looks like. Can you get a ride with Marylou, or do you have your motorbikes out front?"

"Sho nuff," was Tyler's ambiguous answer. He winked at Lawn and sashayed back into the living room.

Art said, "Now that Hunny has money, he's going to put Tyler and Schuyler through medical school. Isn't that great? They plan on becoming podiatrists. They both like feet."

Lawn checked his watch. "Nelson should be arriving soon. There can't be much traffic coming in from Cobleskill this time of night. Of course, it's the weekend, and there are bound to be drunks. Plus people coming down the Northway from the races at Saratoga."

Hunny and Art exchanged glances, and then suddenly Hunny began to tremble. I feared he was having a seizure, but he seemed to know exactly what to do, which was to have another sizeable snort of whatever was in his glass. Then he shuddered once and seemed to exorcise something. After which he began to snuffle quietly as Art pulled Hunny against his shoulder and gently smoothed his little frizz of scraggly hair.

Hunny said tearfully, "Poor Mom, poor Mom."

After a moment, Art said to Lawn and me, "After Hunny's father died at the age of sixty-four of testicular cancer, Mother Van Horn had a rough time of it."

Hunny nodded and shook his head and cried some more.

"Rita had always enjoyed a drink before and after dinner," Art went on. "And to ease her sorrows she — well, let's be frank — Rita started drinking to excess. She had gone to work at Clyde and Arletta Briening's crafts shop as their bookkeeper, and while her imbibing did not immediately affect her work there, it did affect her judgment after hours."

Hunny lowered his head now, and it seemed way too close to the two smoldering cigarettes in his ashtray. Not unaware of the danger, he picked up one of the burning Marlboros and took a drag on it.

Art said, "Mother Rita had always had a nice time playing the ponies at Saratoga, and unfortunately after Carl died she apparently got it in her head that she could help make ends meet with her winnings at the track. One season she had actually come out ahead, and this must have clouded her judgment. But, well, you know how it goes with gambling. Lawn, I suppose you understand, since you are in a similar line of work."

"That's preposterous."

"Anyway, one thing led to another, and apparently pretty soon Mother Rita had begun covering her losses at the track with money she — I'm sorry, Hunny, but I have to say the word — embezzled at Crafts-a-Palooza."

Hunny flinched.

"By the time Arletta and Clyde realized what was going on two years later, Rita had taken sixty-one thousand and some odd dollars from the business. When they confronted her, Rita begged them not to go to the police because it would be so embarrassing for Miriam and Lewis. Hunny, too, but especially Miriam and Lewis, who are active in the Epworth League and other Methodist organizations. Hunny, of course, has a forgiving nature, and also he has always had a soft spot for the criminal element."

"I'm afraid that's true," Hunny said.

"The horrible Brienings unfortunately saw this as an opportunity, and they took it. They knew that Mother Rita would begin collecting over thirteen thousand dollars a year in Social Security in just a couple of months, and they made her sign a letter confessing to stealing their money and agreeing to pay them a thousand dollars a month until the sixty-one thousand had been restored — plus interest. Except, when you figured out the interest, it came to more than two hundred thousand dollars total. So every month Mother Rita's Social Security has been going into her account from the government and then straight out and into Crafts-a-Palooza's account. This has been going on for thirteen years."

Lawn stood looking grim. "I have never heard of any of this. I'm stunned. And I'm sure Nelson couldn't have known either. He would never have put up with extortion. He would have gone to the police, or he would simply have held his nose and paid these people off."

"It's true," Hunny said, "that Miriam and Lewis decided not to tell Nelson. He had always thought so highly of Grandma Rita, and they were afraid it would break his heart. And also it might not be appreciated by Nelson's investment clients that there was a crook in the family. It could have been bad for business."

"A crook in the family that got caught," Art said by way of clarification.

I asked, "How did your mother live, Hunny? With no income to speak of."

"We all helped out. I paid her oil and electric and cable, and Miriam and Lewis dropped off groceries. We all pitched in one time for a new roof. For a number of years Mom worked off and on at McDonald's. Then her mind started slipping a couple of years ago and she became frail at around the same time. She had to get out of the house, so we sold it and that's when we got her into Golden Gardens. The house proceeds paid for the nursing home until that money ran out, and then the home said Mom would have to turn over her Social Security every month. We told the Brienings, and they got mad and said all the money hadn't been paid back yet and they might have to go to the police. That was last month. So I bought two hundred dollars' worth of Instant Warren tickets, hoping I would win and could pay off the Brienings, and — praise de Lawd! — I *did* win."

"But now, apparently," Art said, "the Brienings want half a billion dollars to shut them up, not just what Mother Rita still owes."

Lawn said, "This is just totally bizarre. It's no wonder Nelson is so distraught that he missed a dinner engagement."

"The Brienings have been leaving phone messages since I won the lottery," Hunny said, "but I've just been tossing them in the laundry basket with the other requests. I did mean to get to them, but I thought it wasn't going to hurt if we all did a little partying first and got mellow and the friggin' Brienings could just wait their turn. But they must have gotten antsy and called Nelson. The poor lad. First he has to put up with his rude, crude, proud-to-be-lewd Uncle Hunny, and now he has to deal with these shakedown artists from Cobleskill. The embarrassments for Nelson just keep a-rollin' in, poor sweetie-pie."

The door to the living room opened again, and this time Nelson himself walked through it. He looked frazzled and bordering on the unkempt.

Nelson said, "Uncle Hunny, I don't know if you want to go out there. Probably not. But there are some more TV people out front, and they say they want to interview you and it would be best if you agreed to talk to them."

Hunny looked uncharacteristically nonplussed. "At two in the morning? Who are they? Channel Ten? Channel Thirteen? Channel Six? What is this?"

Nelson said, "They showed me their ID from Focks News in New York. There are two of them — a woman and a cameraman — and they say they're from *The Bill O'Malley Show*."

CHAPTER SIX

"This is a damned impertinence," Hunny said. "Tell them I'll only talk to Anderson Cooper."

"Bill O'Malley is doing a report," Nelson said, "on some organization that wants the lottery commission to take back your winnings because they object to a state agency providing money for immoral purposes. Have you not heard about this? When they told me, my heart just sank."

"Oh, some PR woman from the lottery called this afternoon. She said not to worry, that as long as I was eighteen years old and didn't have a relative who worked for the lottery commission, I was the legal winner. Some other reporters called, too, but they went into the laundry basket."

"These O'Malley people have just driven up from the city, they said. One of your neighbors is an O'Malley viewer and called them and said you were partying and driving everybody in the neighborhood crazy with the noise. I can only begin to imagine how accurate that description was."

"That was earlier. Anyway, what immoral purposes? There's nothing immoral about playing some peppy dance music and throwing a party in your own home."

Lawn said, "I'd be willing to bet that there is a good deal more to it than that."

"It's some religious group," Nelson said. "The Family Preservation Association of Albany County. I told the Focks News people it was too late for an interview, but they said they could see that a party was still going on and they refused to leave. Donald, maybe you are the man to handle this. Would you mind?"

"Normally I don't do press relations."

Art said, "We could send the twins out to talk to them. They could tell about how Hunny is going to put them through medical school."

Lawn shut his eyes, and Nelson said, "Art, I don't believe that will help. Having those two tarts speak for Uncle Hunny is exactly what we do *not* need at this point."

Hunny leaped from his chair and shouted, "Tarts? Tyler and Schuyler are a couple of tarts? Why hasn't anyone told *me* about this? It's the shocker of the century. I think we should get them in here and all sing 'The Battle Hymn of the Republic.'"

"Well, we certainly have to get these O'Malley people out of here," Nelson said, "so that we can discuss a far more difficult matter. Do you know where I have just come from, Uncle Hunny?"

"Lawn told us Cobleskill."

"Yes, Cobleskill. And can you guess who it was I was meeting with out there?"

"I was told it had to do with Mom," Hunny said, and seated himself again and slugged down some more of whatever he was drinking.

Art asked, "Was it the Brienings?"

Nelson looked as if the weight of it all hit him all over again. He said somberly, "Yes. Clyde and Arletta Briening."

"Your parents decided a long time ago not to tell you about them — and about Grandma Rita," Hunny said. "And rightly or wrongly, I went along. They all thought there was no need for you to be hurt. But Grandma Rita is only human, like Art and me, and like you, and like Lawn. And now you know the unfortunate truth."

Lawn looked as though he did not like the sound of some of this, but he kept his mouth shut.

Nelson said, "I am sad for Grandma Rita, that's all. She was devastated by the loss of Grandpa Carl, and in her grief she made a terrible mistake. Now she has paid for this lapse many times over, and other family members have paid also. If I had known, I would have found a way to deal with these wretched people. But now they are completely out of control. They are demanding the insane sum of half a billion dollars. And if they don't receive it, they say, they will make public the letter Grandma Rita signed confessing to stealing sixty-one thousand dollars."

Hunny said, "An incriminating letter. Just like in the Bette Davis movie. Wouldn't you just know?"

I said, "Hunny, what exactly is your mother's mental state at this point? If the embezzlement was revealed, would she even know it?"

"Most days, she would. Others, not so much."

"I have to tell you that I spoke with my parents by phone," Nelson said, "and they think Hunny should pay the five hundred million. They think this would end the whole business with the Brienings and save them a lot of embarrassment in church. I don't agree, and I think we have to find other ways to get rid of the Brienings. Don, you must have dealt with blackmailers before. What's your advice?"

Everyone looked at me. Hunny lit another cigarette.

"Since this is plainly extortion at this point," I said, "I could sit down with them and point out the serious legal consequences of what they are doing. Just laying it all out sometimes is sobering for people like this. There is also the possibility perhaps of negotiating with them. Offer them a hundred thousand or whatever relatively small amount you think you can part with in order to see the end of this. You'd need some kind of legal document signed by them, however, nullifying the agreement Hunny's mother signed. What do they think they are going to do with half a billion dollars anyway? Build Cobleskill's first aircraft carrier, or what?"

"They want part of it to expand Crafts-a-Palooza and open a branch in Albany at the Crossgates Mall. The rest of it, they said, was for what they called their nest egg. They want to retire in a few years, and they want enough for an RV and a house in Tavernier, Florida, where their grandchildren can visit them."

Lawn said, "That sounds like maybe four hundred K. Five at most."

"Maybe," Art said, "we could convince them to take five hundred million worth of tranches."

Hunny couldn't help but chuckle — as he did at nearly everything Art said — but then he remembered something and his face fell. "Tomorrow's my day to visit Mom. The Brienings haven't said anything to her, have they?"

"Not yet," Nelson said. "But part of their threat is simply disgusting. If you don't give them what they're asking for, Uncle Hunny, they say they'll send letters to all the residents at Golden Gardens warning them to be careful of Grandma Rita because she is a thief and people should watch their valuables when she is around."

Hunny clutched his head and shook it. "No, no! Oh, poor Mom! Poor, poor Mom!"

"It's too bad," Art said, his jaw tight, "that these Brienings can't just be…oh, I don't know. Don, in your line of work do you ever play rough with bad guys? Or, if you don't, do you know anybody who might?"

Composing himself, Hunny said, "Art doesn't mean that. Well, he means it, but he's not *really* serious. Anyway, in *The Letter*, it's not the blackmailer that gets killed in the end. It's Bette Davis, who only did what she did out of passionate infatuation. And I don't think any of us want to go down *that* road. No, this situation is different. More like *I am a Fugitive from a Chain Gang*. No offense to Mom."

Nelson said, "The Van Horn family is not the Sopranos. We're going to have to deal with these dreadful people, and we have to be firm with them, but of course we're not going to hurt them physically or otherwise do anything unlawful."

I said, "How do the Brienings think they are going to explain to people their sudden vast wealth? To friends and family, not to mention the IRS?"

"They said they talked to a lawyer in Schenectady, and they can have the money held in a bank in the Cayman Islands. They told me not to be concerned about that, and they would work it out.

They said they saw a report on ABC *20/20* about how people get away with this kind of thing all the time. They said they had worked hard all their lives, and other people were getting away with murder, and now it was their turn to make the system work for them, and it was time for them to clean up."

The wall phone next to Hunny rang, and he picked it up.

"Good evening, Mr. Sands' office. Susie MacNamara speaking. May I help you?"

Hunny listened and said uh-huh several times, and then, "Just a minute." He put his hand over the receiver. "It's the Focks News people out front. They said they know I'm in here and if I don't come out they will stay all night, and sooner or later I'll have to talk to them. Maybe I should say something. They've already interviewed Marylou, and I doubt she told them anything helpful to our situation. Also, they may check and find out she isn't the real Marylou Whitney, and this will only add to all our woes."

Lawn said, "Well, you certainly can't allow them into the house. The place is a pig sty, and there are people in the living room in varying states of undress, and they're looking at some obscene video. It will just be fodder for what this busybody antigay, pro-morality organization is trying to do."

Art said, "It's a great video. *Carnival in Costa Rica.* But it's not the one with Cesar Romero and Vera-Ellen."

Hunny said into the phone, "Give us just another minute, okay?" A few seconds later, he yelped, "Oh no!" and hung up the phone. "They said Marylou invited them into the house for some good weed, and they're on their way in!"

That's when we all heard the sound of a woman's high-pitched shriek.

CHAPTER SEVEN

The Focks cameraman lay on the porch moaning and clutching his chest, and the woman with him was prone behind the porch railing, yelling into her cell phone, "Send the police! Send the police!" The 911 operator must have asked her where she was, because she said, "It's on my GPS! It's in the car on my GPS!"

I asked Hunny to remind us of what his house number on Moth Street was, and he said 126, and the woman yelled into her phone, "One twenty-six Moth Street, in Albany!"

We had all heard a car screech away, but there was no sign of the vehicle by now.

Hunny switched on the porch light, and I looked down at the whimpering young man on the floor. I got on my cell and told 911 that in addition to the police we would need an ambulance.

I said, "Hunny, is anybody in the house a doctor or nurse?" The remaining partygoers were crowded just inside the front door, chattering and peering out.

"No."

The woman with the cell phone came over and said, "Bert! Bert! Don't die on us. Bill needs you. We all need you." She had a hard time bending down because the jeans she was wearing were so tight.

As I got down on my knees to examine the cameraman's soaked T-shirt, I saw with relief that the shooting was not what it first appeared to be. The mess on the man's chest smelled not like blood but like paint. I touched it, and I said, "You've been hit with a paintball pellet. It exploded but it didn't penetrate your body."

"But, hey, this fucking hurts," the cameraman groaned. "I hurt my back. It hurts."

"They tried to kill us!" the woman said. "My God."

"Who fired the paintball? What did you see?"

"I think it was a car. We were just coming up the steps."

Then I remembered that the man dressed as Marylou Whitney had been ushering the newsies into the house, but where was the Saratoga and Palm Beach socialite?

Art had come out now with a flashlight, and he was shining the beam around the porch and the wooden front steps. More red paintballs had struck the porch railing and some of the shingles on the front of the house. A border of marigolds ran along the concrete walkway from the steps down to the sidewalk, also paint-splattered, and it was when Art shone the light down there that we saw the bottom of Marylou's pink gown. Her legs were sticking out from under the forsythia bush below the porch.

Hunny raced down the steps, shouting, "Marylou! Marylou!"

A muffled voice came out from under the bush. "Hunny, I'm stuck. I fell off the steps, and my necklace is caught on something."

"Oh, girl, you look like the Wicked Witch of the West and the house fell on you."

"Somebody shot a gun."

"But it was just paint, Donald says. Were you hit? Are you wounded?"

"I don't know, darling."

Now the woman in the tight jeans was on her cell phone again, and I heard her say something about "they tried to kill us" and "a transvestite may have set us up."

I asked Art for his flashlight and then crawled under the bush to find out what was holding onto Marylou. Her diamond necklace had become entangled on a forsythia branch, and while she aimed the flashlight I broke off bits of the branch and tried to free the Whitney jewels without damaging them further.

Marylou said, "I know we have known each other for such a short, short time, but I have to tell you, whoever you are, that I think I am falling in love."

"Okey-dokes."

She had scratches on her neck and jaw and her wig was seriously askew, but Marylou did not seem to have been hit with a paint pellet.

"You're sure you're okay?" I asked.

"I am feeling a bit moist, but that may be from the excitement."

I yelled, "She seems to be uninjured. We'll be with you in a second."

Hunny said, "Maybe the attackers will be back. Oh, where are the Albany police when you need them!"

There was a sudden brightness, and as Marylou and I wriggled free of the forsythia and I helped her to her feet, I saw the woman in the tight jeans wielding a video camera with a light atop it and recording our struggles. Apparently this would be Marylou's debut on Focks News, and mine also.

I said, "I heard you speculating on who the paint shooter was after. It's a safe bet that they were not shooting at you but at Hunny or Art or their friends. No one even knew you were here."

"Who are you?" she snapped. "I need a name please. And your position here."

"Don Strachey. I'm a private investigator working for Hunny. Billionaires attract bad people occasionally, and that's why I am present. Based on your remarks on the phone just now, it sounds to me as if you are among the bad people Hunny needs to be protected from."

"I'm Jane Trinkus and I don't need lectures from you on how to do my job. If Bill was here, he would make short work of a dickhead like you. As his representative, I am telling you to watch out or I will do the same."

"I'm making a note."

There were no sirens, but the cop car that turned off Transformer came up Moth Street fast, flashing like a meteor.

Art said, "Finally, Alice Blue Gown."

There were plenty of parking places along the street, but the patrol car double parked and two officers got out. "Who made the 911 call?" the older one asked.

Trinkus identified herself as a producer for *The Bill O'Malley Show* and said, "We know that we are not liked in the homosexual community, but this is the first time anyone actually tried to kill us. My cameraman Bert Spatz is lying on the porch severely wounded, and I am just lucky to be alive."

The cop indicated to his junior officer to go up and check on the cameraman, while Hunny said, "Somebody shot paint pellets from a car and raced off. Very *noir*-ish, even without the fog and other cheesy effects. But I don't think they were shooting at these Bill O'Malley lovelies. I won the lottery this week, and I've had nothing but trouble since then. I have a private detective, in fact, Don Strachey here, who is looking into a number of unfortunates who have shown up since Wednesday."

The cop acknowledged me with a nod but was more interested in Hunny. "So you're Huntington Van Horn?"

"I'm afraid so."

"Congratulations, sir. Yes, I've heard of this happening. Lottery winners are shown on TV, and then people start bothering them and trying to walk off with a piece of the winnings, legally or illegally."

Now Trinkus was on the phone again with somebody, saying, "We may be in danger. The cops up here are in bed with the gays. Maybe somebody should wake Bill up. This is incredible!"

There were more flashing lights, and an ambulance rolled up the street and halted behind the police cruiser. A young man and a young woman in uniform got out quickly and the cop pointed to the porch.

The officer, a Sergeant Filio, took statements from everyone who had witnessed the paintball attack. Trinkus stuck to her theory that the Focks News crew were "shot at" by radical gays, probably people who Hunny phoned and alerted that Focks News was about to ambush him. The officer said he just wanted a narrative of what actually happened, and when, and he said detectives would soon arrive to question witnesses and listen to any ideas they had on who might have done the shooting.

After Marylou gave her version of events, the cop said, "Mrs. Whitney, you probably shouldn't leave Saratoga without some kind of security whenever you are wearing your jewels."

"Oh, officer, thank you so much for such sound advice."

Trinkus said, "That's not Marylou Whitney. It's a fucking drag queen. Are you serious?"

Sergeant Filio said, "I'm just going to pretend I never heard that," and winked at Marylou.

The cop turned his attention to the EMTs, who were now hauling the cameraman down the steps on a gurney, and Art said to Hunny under his breath, "I know that cop. He used to date Malcolm Thibidoux."

"Where are you taking him?" Trinkus yelled after the EMTs as they slid the gurney into the ambulance, and they told her Albany Medical Center.

"Is he going to be okay?"

"Should be. He says his back hurts. Probably from when he fell over. But the paint didn't get in his eyes or anything"

"Be brave, Bert, be brave," she called after him. "Bill will be so supportive of you."

Another police car arrived as the ambulance was pulling away, and two plainclothes officers led us through our recitations a second time. Again, Jane Trinkus speculated that she and her cohorts had been shot at by "gay terrorists."

Hunny and I had a quick, private back-and-forth as to whether we should mention to the detectives Stu Hood, Mason Doebler and Hunny's several other assorted boyfriends and tricks who had made vague or specific threats over the past three days. We decided not to. Hunny said, "They're not all model citizens, but now that I am a billionaire I guess I can deal with them on my own, no? With your help, Donald, I mean. And if any of these lads turns out to be into paintball wars, you can hand him over to the girls in blue. Why stir up trouble for these unfortunate youths, many of whom are practically middle-aged by now, and perfectly harmless?"

I guessed what Hunny was also saying was, let's not go poking a stick into the busy hive of his sexual past, for God knew what else might come buzzing out to chase Hunny up and down his hectic erotic landscape. Keeping this part of his life separate for the moment and away from the police did seem to make sense. Especially given that Hunny had so many people angry at him at this point that focusing on a few unstable tricks and rent boys just felt laughably limited.

CHAPTER EIGHT

"Well, at least Hunny's not on *Meet the Press*," Timmy said, indicating the kitchen television set. "Not yet."

He had one eye on two Sunday morning health-care-debate talking heads, another eye on the *Times Union* spread out on the kitchen table, and a third eye — I was always amazed that he could do this — on his masala tea, a relic of his long-ago Peace Corps days, that was busy coagulating in a large mug that sat between us. I was having coffee and an English muffin, and I was fretting over Tom Friedman's dark forecasts in the *Times*. Global warming, with its inundated cities and wars over vanishing natural resources, was a good momentary distraction from Hunny.

"These people are just bonkers," Timmy said, as he read the *TU* page one story on the Family Preservation Association of Albany County. "They can't actually believe that the Lottery Commission might take back Hunny's billion dollars. But they are having a high old time making lottery officials squirm, and they're getting all kinds of ink for their screwball organization while they're at it."

"Ink is who they are."

"And of course Hunny is a godsend."

"He is a bit of a right-wing gay caricature. If Hunny hadn't existed, Rush Limbaugh would have had to invent him. It's why I think I'm basically glad to be working for him. I mean, in addition to walking away with a tiny portion of his billion dollars. In a world of gay folks like us who are busily turning queer life in America into a kind of insipid parody of our parents' dull, stable existences, Hunny is this horrifying creature climbing out of the primordial homo ooze. I have to say that I find him alternately hair-raising and beguiling."

"Insipid? Donald, do you think our life is insipid?"

"No, I like it. It's nice. It's comfortable. I wouldn't have it any other way."

"Then what are you saying? Would our lives — and the lives of our gay friends who are like us — be improved if we were all more like Hunny and Art and that gay menagerie they surround themselves with?"

"No. But you know I like to quote Ogden Nash. 'Home is heaven, and orgies are vile, but I like an orgy once in a while.' You've even been known to quote him yourself in recent years. If not in Albany, then certainly from time to time on vacation in Thailand."

He pretended to bristle, then laughed. "Of course we all have a streak of Hunny in us, expressed or unexpressed. But it's the *flaunting* — there, I said the right-wingers' word — it's the flaunting of this life of booze and boys and mayhem that just gets tiresome. And, yes, embarrassing. There, I said that, too. In the straight world, people like Hunny make me embarrassed to be gay."

"Me too. Except I'm kind of embarrassed to be embarrassed."

"Yes, you would be. I'd like to be. But I can't. I'm just embarrassed."

"The *TU* story doesn't mention any gay groups in Albany or elsewhere coming to Hunny's defense. That's disappointing. I guess they're embarrassed, too."

"With his billion dollars," Timmy said, "Hunny probably doesn't need any help. He can hire all the help he needs. Like you."

"Me, and he's getting a lawyer to deal with the DeCarlo lawsuit. Plus, we agreed that after last night's paintball episode he should hire some private security people for his house. I put him in touch with Gray Security, and they should have some people over there by now."

"You said it was unclear who the paint shooter this morning was trying to hit. Only the TV people and the Marylou Whitney impersonator were on the front steps at the time. But isn't it possible that somebody who hates Hunny just took some potshots at the house, and they didn't care who they hit? They just wanted to frighten Hunny and complicate his life?"

"That's what it looks like. And maybe with a little luck, humiliate a few fags. Not knowing that the Bill O'Malley people were in the line of fire."

"I am guessing that we haven't heard the last of Focks News. I'm sure O'Malley will call for the death penalty."

"This is a job for the Albany PD, and all the indications are they'll take it seriously. They know that paint is only paint, but those war-game pellets can do real harm to people who aren't wearing vests and goggles. What happened last night was assault, and the cops I met seem prepared to treat it that way."

"Wouldn't it be interesting," Timmy said, "if the paintball attack could be traced back to one of the Family Preservation people. FPAAC is up to its eyebrows in local conservative wing-nuts — tea-baggers, birthers, deathers and other types of Obama haters."

"Except, when Second Amendment crazies lose control, they tend not to just shoot paint. They go in with real Uzis and go down in a blaze of glory taking as many people with them as they can. This thing feels more like a homophobic out-of-control loony or drunk."

"So, Donald, what exactly is your role at this point? The police will investigate the paint attack and the security people will protect Hunny. What will you be doing to earn your fee?"

"There are still a few of Hunny's former occasional and short-term boyfriends I need to check out. Guys who have sent threatening notes or phone messages."

"By short-term, I suppose you mean ranging from several hours down to ten minutes."

"Yes, speed dating seems to be one of Hunny's favorite pastimes."

"And these Briening people. Surely you can be helpful dealing with them. You've dealt with extortionists before — though none that I can recall who were quite as grandiose in their expectations as the Brienings."

"I'm trying to figure out whether the Brienings' delusional venality will be an advantage or a disadvantage. Lack of rationality is generally an obstacle in situations like this, but these people are so off the wall that I may mau-mau them and they'll just go poof. Anyway, I should soon get an inkling as to what I am dealing with. I'm going to drive out to Cobleskill this afternoon."

Something somebody was saying on *Meet the Press* caught Timmy's attention, and then my cell phone went off.

"Strachey."

"Don, I need your help," Hunny said, his voice shaky. "Can you drive over to East Greenbush? Art and I came out to Golden Gardens to see Mom. But she's gone."

Gone? "Hunny, do you mean that your mother has passed away?" This could solve certain problems.

"No, she's just *not here*. And nobody knows where Mom *went*."

I said I'd be there in ten minutes.

∫ ∫ ∫ ∫

"They say they're going to have to notify the police," Hunny said. "They're searching the premises one more time, and if Mom doesn't turn up they are going to have to call the sheriff's office. I'm thinking maybe they shouldn't wait. I mean, they found her wheelchair by the front door, for heaven's sake. It sounds like she somehow just *left*. Got out the door and wandered away somewhere."

"There's a receptionist," I pointed out. "Or isn't she always at her desk?"

Art said, "We've come in here when she's back out of sight in the office, catching some zees, or trimming her nose hairs, or whatever."

"Mom rides around in that chair — she calls it her taxi to nowhere — but she can walk in her slow, rickety way. There was nothing to prevent her from strolling right out the door and —

what? Hitching a ride to almost anyplace."

"The other doors are alarmed," Art said, "but not the front."

"What was she wearing when she was last seen?"

"Just her bathrobe and slippers. Mom has been meticulous about her appearance all her life. Or she was until recently. She might not have been aware that she was dressed somewhat inappropriately for appearing in public."

I was standing and Hunny and Art were seated on a bench in the corridor outside the administrator's office. Elderly men and women in various stages of inert disrepair were slumped in wheelchairs up and down the hallway. Some had looked up at me as I walked in, but most took no notice. The place was decorated with pretty-posy wall stencils, under the apparent assumption that none of the inmates would have found Motherwell interesting or gotten a charge out of a Munch or two. The hall we were in did not smell fetid, but the stench of disinfectant was not much of a substitute.

"I talked to Mom yesterday afternoon," Hunny said, "and she told me how much she was looking forward to my visit. The staff here had told Mom about me winning the lottery even before I called her on Thursday, so I guess everybody here knew I was coming. And I told Mrs. Kerisiotis, the administrator, that I would donate new flat-screen TVs to all the rooms. That went over big, and I have to say, it went through my mind that Mom might get a little extra TLC as a result."

Art said, "Hunny also offered to have the dietician sent on a long trip to Hawaii and replaced by somebody who could cook, but nobody here has said any more about that."

"Was yesterday afternoon the last time you spoke to your mother?" I asked.

"Not long after I got home from your office."

"And she sounded normal?"

"Normal? Well, normal for Mom in the past couple of years is not exactly what Dr. Joyce Brothers would call normal.

Sometimes she's her good old self. Other times she forgets things and people. And she gets frustrated and mad. A couple of weeks ago one of the nurses told me that Mom had thrown her Depends at an aide and told people to stop treating her like a baby. I asked her about this, but she said she didn't remember doing it, and we both had a good laugh over that one."

Hunny and Art both stood up as a tiny middle-aged woman wearing a blue business suit, a pink ruffled collar and a huge brooch that looked like a sea urchin came striding up the corridor.

"That's Mrs. Kerisiotis," Hunny said. "When Mom went missing, she came in, even though it's Sunday."

I was introduced by name but not title or function, and Mrs. Kerisiotis said to Hunny, "Did you telephone your mother early this morning, Huntington?"

"No, I didn't."

"Your mother's roommate, Nola Conklin, says your mom received a phone call at about a quarter of eight. Nola was half asleep and she couldn't make out what was said. It wasn't long after that that Rita left the room in her wheelchair. She was dressed only in her nightie and bathrobe, so of course any staff seeing her headed down the hall would have thought she was going in the direction of the lounge or the game room. Can you ask around among friends and relatives and try to find out who might have phoned her?"

"Yes, I will do that. Oh God."

"Huntington, there is still no sign of your mother, and I think I will have to notify the sheriff's department. Some of our staff have even walked up and down the highway asking if any neighbors might have noticed your mum, but no one reported seeing her. I am so, so sorry this has happened. I think that Rita may have been determined to leave the building, and cleverly she took advantage of the front desk shift change at eight o'clock. She has certainly never done such a thing before. Has she talked to you at all about wanting to leave Golden Gardens or of wanting to go to a particular place?"

"No," Hunny said. "Mom has always said this place suits her. I mean, she says it's boring and smells bad and the food is revolting and sometimes she feels like she would just as soon be rotting in a grave as rotting in a nursing home. But she says most of the staff are nice, and the heating system works fine in the winter."

"Yes, she seems to like it here, and Rita is well-liked by both the staff and the other residents. Now, Mrs. Conklin told me your mom became agitated while watching the six o'clock news on TV yesterday evening. I know that you have been in the news, and I am wondering if she may have become upset over a report on you and your lottery prize and these Albany people who are trying to have your prize revoked. Did she not mention anything about this to you?"

Hunny looked stricken and reached for his cigarettes and then quickly put them back. "No, but she means to tell me things and then things slip her mind. She has mentioned that this happens. So she might have seen me being maligned by those religious nut cases and she decided to give them a piece of her mind or something. That would be just like Mom."

"Mother Rita is a cheerful lady who likes to have her bit of fun," Art said. "But she doesn't suffer fools, either."

Hunny said, "I wonder if she went to find the FPAAC people and tell them off. But how would she even know who they were or where to find them? Now I'm *really* worried. Maybe the sheriff's people could look for her wherever the FPAAC idiots are. Do they have an office, or a den, or a nest, or what? And Donald, girl, you could check out FPAAC, too, and maybe infiltrate them or keep an eye on them or something."

"I'll add them to my list. This afternoon I may visit the Brienings in Cobleskill. But if your Mom doesn't turn up soon, she'll be my first priority."

Hunny grabbed his cigarettes and in the same motion jammed them back in his shirt pocket. "I almost forgot about the putrid Brienings. Good grief, maybe they *kidnapped* Mom. Called her up and lured her outside and then whisked her away!"

Art said, "Why would they do that, luv?"

"Oh, I don't know. Because I'm rich and famous. Like when those people snatched Frank Sinatra Junior or the Getty kid."

"But those were for the ransom. The Brienings don't need Mother Rita to extort money from you. They've got that letter instead."

Mrs. Kerisiotis said, "Who are the Brienings?"

I could all but see the wheels spinning inside Hunny's head and the terror he felt over the possibility of his mother's being revealed in Golden Gardens as a thief. He said, "They're people Mom had some trouble with a long time ago. It was an argument over a breaded zucchini recipe."

"It's hard to imagine your mother having a long-standing disagreement with anyone, Huntington. She is generally such a cheery lady. She can be outspoken, of course, and she has her opinions. And she doesn't like to be bothered with Depends. But five minutes after she lets off steam, she is back to being as sweet as can be. The aides all love Rita. She tells them stories that I would consider off-color, but the staff all think she is just a hoot."

Tears welled in Hunny's eyes. "That's my mom."

Now the large-breasted black man with a heavy beard and glittering earring who Timmy and I had seen on television at Hunny's winning-the-lottery party came down the corridor in a green nurse's outfit. His cornucopia of rhinestones still dangled from his left ear.

Hunny shouted, "Antoine!" and the two embraced and Art soon joined in the hug.

"Hunny, honey, we can't find your mom, but I'm sure she is somewhere okay. That Rita can take care of herself, girl. You better believe it!"

"Oh, Antoine, honey, where in the world would Mom go? It sounds like she knew what she was doing — snuck out during the front desk shift change. Or maybe it wasn't premeditated, and it was just a moment of opportunity and she took it. But Mrs. Kerisiotis says you all have looked high and low, and now she's going to call the sheriff. Oh God, please don't let the police find her dead in a drainage ditch being gnawed on by wild dogs!"

This image seemed to spur the administrator to action, and Mrs. Kerisiotis headed into her office making speaking-into-a-receiver gestures.

"Hunny, honey, your mom is just such a dear lady, and I'm sure she is going to be back here where she belongs in no time at all."

"Oh, Antoine, honey, I am trying to believe that."

"Rita told us a joke the other day that had us all rolling on the floor and screaming our heads off. Did she tell you the one about the lady who led a cute bag boy out to the supermarket parking lot? The lady says to the bag boy, 'I'm glad you came outside with me. I have to tell you, I have an itchy pussy.' The humpy kid says to the lady, 'Well, you're going to have to point it out to me. All those Japanese cars look alike.'"

Hunny and Art's laughter was so rollicking that several of the old folks staring at the floor in the corridor looked up.

"I know Mom gets on the phone with her old friend Tex Clermont once a week to trade jokes."

"Hunny, I sure do see where you get your sense of humor."

"Antoine, Mom has had a nice time here overall. Minus the disgusting food and so on. So I can't begin to imagine why she would just walk out the door. It's true, her mind is going."

"I've noticed that, Hunny. But she has two or three marbles left, and on a good day she's one hundred percent. Well, eighty-two."

"Maybe she just went for a stroll. It's such a sunny day out. It's kind of hot, but Mom has never minded the heat. Or she walked down to Dairy Queen for a treat."

"We all checked down there. But don't you fret, Hunny. Those girls in the sheriff's department will have her back here in no time at all. One time a lady made it out the door and three miles down Route 43, and the officers found her in the waiting room at Jiffy Lube reading the *Troy Record*. She said she liked it there because the coffee at Jiffy Lube was better than the coffee at Golden Gardens. That poor lady — her name was Turalura Butterworth — passed away a week after the sheriff brought her back here. But that was just a coincidence, I am certain."

Now Mrs. Kerisiotis came back out from her office. She said two sheriff's deputies were on their way, and they would get word out to all patrol officers in the region about the missing Golden Gardens resident. When Mrs. Kerisiotis told the duty officer the name of the missing patient, he had said to her, "Van Horn? Why is that name sounding familiar?"

"Huntington," Mrs. Kerisiotis said, "you are such a celebrity. The next thing you know I'll go into the Grand Union and your face will be on the cover of the *National Inquirer*. We'll find out all about your hidden secrets and scandalous love life."

Mrs. Kerisiotis grinned, but Hunny only smiled back feebly.

CHAPTER NINE

The noontime sun was brilliant and the air steamy, and I cranked the AC as I sped down the interstate toward Cobleskill.

It seemed unlikely that the Brienings were in any way connected to the disappearance of Rita Van Horn. She was most valuable to them settled comfortably among her unknowing and potentially judgmental fellow residents at Golden Gardens. But I needed to talk with them anyway about their crude extortion plot, so it wasn't going to hurt to gauge their reaction to Mrs. Van Horn's having gone AWOL.

Hunny, meanwhile, was phoning family members and his mother's friends and acquaintances to find out if any of them knew of her whereabouts. And the East Greenbush Fire Department was preparing to launch a volunteer ground search if Mrs. Van Horn had not been found by mid-afternoon.

I had never been to Cobleskill. It was one of the small towns off I-88 heading west toward the southern tier counties, about forty-five minutes from Albany. It had a thriving agricultural college that was part of the State University of New York system, and as I headed into town from the interstate the place didn't have that woebegone feeling of so many upstate burgs whose original industrial reasons for existing had long since migrated to Central America and Asia.

My GPS led me to Crafts-a-Palooza in a strip mall in the west end of town. The Brienings had a place the width of two storefronts, and the vacant, former used bookstore next door looked like the spot where they might be planning their multi-million-dollar mega-expansion. I had a tuna sub at the Subway store at the other end of the mall, and when I walked outside and the sun pounded down on me I was sorry I had eaten the whole thing. I wasn't going to be as alert with the Brienings as I wanted to be, not that I was under the impression that dealing with them was going to require subtlety.

The place was busy with Sunday afternoon young and old women perusing the paints, beads, sparkles, plastic water lilies the size of bed pans, and unpainted plaster dwarfs. There were front yard windmills whose vanes had the Ten Commandments printed on them and in the middle a picture of a smiling Sarah Palin. I had never set foot in an extruded-yard-novelty factory in Taipei, but I imagined that if I ever went there it would smell just like the Crafts-a-Palooza store in Cobleskill, New York.

A checkout clerk told me that Arletta and Clyde didn't ordinarily come into the store on Sundays, but they happened to be nearby. They were next door in the former used bookstore taking measurements. I asked if that was because Crafts-a-Palooza was expanding, and the clerk said yes, probably in the early fall.

I hadn't noticed the Brienings inside the defunct bookshop because the lights weren't on, but I soon spotted them in the dim recesses at the rear. I shoved the front door open and walked in and they both looked my way, startled.

"Yes?"

"Mrs. Briening?"

"Yes?"

They both gave me a sour-faced once-over.

"I'm Donald Strachey, a private investigator. My client, Huntington Van Horn, suggested that we talk."

Four eyes narrowed at the mention of Hunny's name.

"A private detective?" Clyde said. "My wife and I have nothing to say to you. If we talk to any detective, it will be a detective on the New York State Police."

"Now, we're busy," Arletta said, "and, Mr. Detective, I think you need to just scoot on out of here."

They were both tiny rail-thin people with tiny rail-thin faces and mean gray eyes. Both their complexions were the texture and color of zinc. She had on blue slacks and a white blouse with big orange polka dots on it, and he was wearing Nantucket red golf pants and a tan sport shirt and had colored his hair with what looked like steak sauce.

I said, "Extortion is a class-A felony in the state of New York. If you keep on scamming Hunny's mother, instead of spending your golden years in the Florida Keys, you may wind up spending them in Sing Sing. That is what I have driven out here to emphasize to you. Maybe up until now you have not been obliged to think about what you have done in those terms. But now I hope you will think about it with care. I'll bet you would much rather have your grandchildren running up to you and showing you the pretty seashells they found at the beach down in Tavernier than pressing their noses up against a filthy plexiglass shield in Ossining with the two of you on the other side of it sobbing."

They both looked at me as if I were brainless, and she said, "Rita Van Horn is an embezzler. She is lucky she isn't in Sing Sing herself. It is only out of the goodness of our hearts that we didn't have that woman sent straight to jail. As for any idea of extortion, as you call it, you are just full of it, fella. We possess a legal document, signed by Rita Van Horn, stipulating repayment of the money she stole from Clyde and myself. The agreement contains clauses for penalties and interest, and the only thing Clyde and I have done in recent days is invoke a few of those clauses. And if you think I am bluffing, well, then we will just see you in court! So, how do you like *them* apples, Mr. Albany Private Investigator?"

It occurred to me that I had never laid eyes on the infamous letter, and I wondered if Hunny or anyone else had. Or had they just taken the word of Hunny's mother that she had signed such a document?

I said, "That letter is worthless, and I think you know it is. It's an informal agreement with no force of law. You're just a couple of con artists, and I am here to tell you that your con is over as of this minute. Mrs. Van Horn has repaid you many times over for the money she took. And the idea that you might extract some absurd additional sum from her or her newly wealthy son is just plain nuts."

"So," Clyde said coolly, "do you think Rita doesn't particularly care if the folks out at Golden Gardens find out that she is a criminal? And that woman *is* a thief. We're doing them all a favor by keeping her from committing additional crimes. In fact, we told her straight out that as long as she doesn't steal money from folks in the nursing home, or any of the staff — and as long as she keeps up with the make-good payments to Arletta and myself — we won't notify the residents that they have a dangerous klepto lurking right there among them."

"We just wrote to Rita on Thursday," Arletta said. "And she must have received our letter by now. I'm not surprised she hasn't shown it to you or probably to anybody else. She is up to her eyebrows in shame, shame, shame. As well she should be. Clyde and I sent her a Xerox of her agreement with us, and we let her know that we have other copies we will be compelled to send to the Albany County district attorney's office if we are not repaid soon. And I mean compensated both for our financial losses and for the pain and suffering we endured when we lost not only sixty-one thousand dollars but also our sense of trust, which was betrayed so sickeningly. Clyde and I used to be trusting people, and now we have become more cynical. It is not just our money that Rita Van Horn stole, but our innocence."

These people were both calculating and delusional, and it was becoming clear that the worst they were likely to do was shame and embarrass an old lady whose additional years of experiencing embarrassment and moral shame were limited. But they weren't limited quite enough. Mother Rita was, according to Hunny's friend Antoine, still eighty-two percent there on some days. And she apparently cared what people thought of her, as did her family — Hunny, his sister Miriam and her husband Lewis. Nelson, who had hooked up with a man who dealt in tranches and derivatives, seemed ready to forgive and forget and to be more philosophical about swindling the unwary. Not so, the more orthodox-Methodist Van Horns, and not so Hunny, who seemed willing to do almost anything to keep his adored and adoring mother from being humiliated, if not hauled into court.

The store room we were standing around arguing in was uncomfortably hot without air-conditioning. It occurred to me to invite the Brienings over to the nearby Subway outlet for a cool drink, and where I might shove both of these vicious little creeps into the cooler compartment, if Subway had one, and jam the door shut. But they might not die. They might wrap themselves in coats made of doughy sub buns and survive on American cheese. And I would be convicted of attempted murder.

So instead I said, "Rita Van Horn is missing from the nursing home. She left this morning around eight, and no one knows what has become of her. A search has been organized. If you wrote her a letter that precipitated some kind of emotional crisis in Rita, you will bear a heavy responsibility for whatever has happened to her."

They gawked. "Nobody escapes from those places," Clyde said. "Rita must be hiding on the premises."

Arletta added, "Have they checked the bookkeeper's office? If the safe is in there, where they keep the residents' valuables, that would be the first place I would look."

I said, "Do you people seriously believe that Hunny Van Horn might actually turn over half a billion dollars to you?"

"We not only believe it," Arletta said, "we are counting on it. We are expanding our store here in the fall, and we have been in touch with Crossgates about leasing space at the mall. In addition, as we told Nelson, we are planning to build a lovely retirement home in Florida. And — not that it is any of business of yours — we plan to make a major contribution to an excellent organization in Albany that is protesting the lottery commission paying out all that taxpayer money to a man as immoral as Hunny Van Horn."

"You're talking about FPAAC?"

Looking smug, Arletta said, "You betcha."

"But if the lottery commission revokes Hunny's winnings, you won't get a dime."

Clyde stood looking serene, and Arletta smirked some more. "Well, of course they aren't going to take Hunny's billion dollars back. The lottery commission is run by a bunch of big-government liberals who support the radical homosexual agenda. So I am confident that Hunny will keep his billion dollars, and I am just as confident that Clyde and I are going to end up with our fair share. That would be half."

I said, "Of course, if something bad has happened to Rita Van Horn, you people are up the creek."

"Has she really run off?" Clyde asked, looking nervous.

The two of them stood watching me with sudden apprehension, and that's when I concluded that even if they hadn't snatched her, the letter they had sent her renewing their threats had shoved Mrs. Van Horn into some awful tailspin that was likely to end up badly hurting her as well as everyone else involved.

CHAPTER TEN

Back at the house on Moth Street, Hunny sat by the kitchen table chain-smoking. He gazed up longingly at the wall phone as if he might will it to ring and someone on the other end of the line would happily announce that Rita Van Horn was safe and sound. In anticipation of such a call, Hunny had sent out for champagne and clam dip. Nelson and Lawn had come by briefly and then driven over to join Hunny's sister Miriam and her husband Lewis at Golden Gardens, the epicenter of the search.

Friends had gathered at Hunny and Art's house to offer comfort. Schuyler and Tyler were there, off in a corner where Marylou Whitney was helping them with their homework. They were students at Hudson Valley Community College, Art told me, and were planning to switch their major from corporate communications to pre-med since Hunny had offered to finance their educations.

Mrs. Whitney, whose real name, Art confided to me, was Guy Snyder and who was an accountant in the New York State Department of Taxation, was also serving as press liaison. For word had spread that the aged mother of the lottery billionaire had gone missing and reporters were gathering out front on the sidewalk. Among them was a crew from Focks News that included the field producer Jane Trinkus, as well as a new cameraman and two armed bruisers from the Focks security department in New York. They spent much of their time palavering with the two Gray Security guards Hunny had hired at my suggestion. The wounded cameraman was still under treatment at Albany Med and was said to be recovering from his back injury. Trinkus had told Hunny that Bill O'Malley himself might be coming up to Albany, and Hunny should consider having an attorney present for the interview.

Other media representatives had also been in touch, Hunny told me, including a man from the All-Too-Real Channel who had seen Hunny on *The Today Show* and wanted to talk to him about doing a reality show. Cameras would be installed around the house, the man said, and Hunny and Art would live normally except for the addition of some "plot points," such as screaming matches over who had left the shower curtain outside the tub and jealous fits over either Hunny or Art coming on to a UPS man. Hunny had also been contacted by someone from a gay cable channel called Oh Look! TV about the channel's doing a movie of Hunny's life. A writer from the network had already called and said he planned on dramatizing Hunny's experiences in the first Gulf War and his encounters with vampires.

I said, "Hunny, were you actually in the military?"

"Define *in.*"

Art said, "When we lived in New York, a soldier who hung out at the Stonewall used to drive us over to Fort Dix and sneak us in to cheer up the troops. That's how Fort Dix got its name. Hunny and I named it."

"We thought about calling it Fort Cox."

"Or, if the Army found that too risqué, Fort Erection."

"I don't see how they can say gays in the military would be bad for morale," Hunny added. "From what we saw, having a few pecker lovers around can be *excellent* for morale. The fighters in the Taliban should be so lucky."

"I'm surprised," I said, "that none of your old Stonewall pals have turned up in recent days to lend support. Or maybe just looking for a handout like so many others."

"A few have called with congratulations," Hunny said. "But so many of the vets have passed on. Not many made it through the eighties and the plague. And of course there are the ones who are now major CEOs or archbishops or whatever who would never let on that in 1968 they liked getting fucked in the toilet at the Stonewall or blew the NYPD sergeants who came in for their weekly payoffs."

Art said, "We haven't heard either from the ten thousand people who said they were there that night but actually weren't.

Or from the ones who stood on the other side of Christopher Street in nicely dressed little groups going tsk-tsk-tsk, why are these tawdry queens misbehaving like this, why don't these embarrassing lowlifes go home and write their congressman?"

I was not quite old enough to have been there, but I sometimes wondered where I would have stood on that June night that ignited the post '50s and '60s gay rights movement, had I been present. Would I have joined the drunken kick line that sang "We are the Stonewall girls" and hurled bottles and debris at the rampaging cops? Fat chance. Or would I have been among the contemptuous better-heeled gay bystanders across the street muttering about how grossly impolite and impolitic the rebellion was? I'd like to think I would have been among the organizers who moved in, in the following days, to set up more focused and orderly protests, and who initiated the legal challenges that led to the police and other reforms of the seventies and eighties. But maybe I would not yet have been sufficiently clear-headed about myself and brave enough to do even that.

Hunny said, "We're in touch with a couple of the old Stonewall gang, but that all feels like ancient history when what you're basically thinking about is getting up every day and going to work and making the car payments and dealing with mom and maybe getting a little man-nookie once in a while."

"Hourly," Art said.

"You guys seem to have a really busy and varied sex life," I said. "Or is a lot of that just talk? Or wishful thinking?"

"We try not to let it be," Hunny said. "It does keep a girl on her toes making sure her tubes remain cleared. Artie and I manage, though, don't we, girl?"

I asked, "And this way of life has not been problematical?"

Art looked puzzled. "In what way?"

"Oh, the usual. Disease. Legal difficulties. Getting involved with people who turn out to be crazy or dangerous."

"Oh, girl! All of the above. Why else would *you* be sitting here, Donald?"

This reminded me that I still had to check out a few of the blackmailers and extortionists who had turned up late in the week. I had told Hunny and Art that I had not gotten far with the Brienings during my visit to Cobleskill, but that I had learned of a letter they had sent to Rita Van Horn. Hunny called his friend Antoine at Golden Acres and asked him to make a discreet search of Mrs. Van Horn's room and to pocket the letter and bring it to Hunny after work. Antoine called back and said he had the letter and would deliver it around four-thirty.

The phone rang and Hunny snatched it up. After a moment, he said, "Well, thank you, dear. No, no word yet. Okay, you stay in touch, girl."

He hung up and said, "That's my cousin, Wesley Bump. He checked with Aunt Joycelyn, and Mom never called her. She doesn't seem to have contacted anybody in the family about what she's up to. Oh Lord, I just know that poor Mom has been having one of her days where she's not all there, and she's probably somewhere where people think she's a local derelict. But what gets me is, why don't people see this old lady going around in her bathrobe and call the police? Why can't they see that she is in need of assistance?"

The phone rang several more times over the next half hour, and at one point Hunny had a CNN producer on call-waiting while he talked to a reporter from Albany's Channel Ten. He told all news people the same thing: Mrs. Van Horn was still missing and he begged anyone who knew of her whereabouts to contact the East Greenbush sheriff's office. He described his mother as "the sweetest old gal you'd ever want to run across" and a "real live wire" who everybody thought the world of.

Just after four-thirty, Antoine arrived and Hunny and Art both leaped up to hug him.

Hunny began to weep, and said, "Oh Antoine, girl, I am trying to hold out hope, but I'm afraid I might be losing it. I don't know how much more of this suspense I can take. I feel like Doris Day in *The Man Who Knew Too Much*. I keep wanting to sing 'Que Sera, Sera' and then wait for Mom to join in from upstairs somewhere,

where she's being held captive. But we already looked in all the rooms on the second floor and up in the attic, and we're certain that Mom isn't here in the house."

"Oh, Hunny, honey, you can't lose it, girl! You have to be a tower of strength. Now, not to worry. The fire department, they've got about thirty folks out combing the woods and fields, and they have two church groups coming over in a little bit, Baptists and your sister Miriam's Methodist ladies. The Presbyterians all went home to start supper, but some of them who got word will be praying for your mom. I am sure that dear lady is going to turn up any minute now, and we're all going to just howl at the stories she has to tell."

"I want to believe that. I want so badly to believe that."

Art said, "Did you bring the letter?"

"I hope this is the right one. Hunny, you said it was from Cobleskill, and the one I brought is the only one with a Cobleskill return address. I didn't look inside, as you said you preferred that I don't. Anyway, how come? Is it blackmail or something?"

"Why would you ask that?" Hunny said.

"I don't know. You've got all sorts of shady stuff in your past. Maybe your mom does, too. Like mother, like son."

"Where would you get that idea?"

"Hunny, honey, I'm not saying it's the same thing. That your mom has sucked half the dicks in Albany County, plus Schenectady and Rensselaer, too, or like that. It could be something else."

Hunny looked stunned, and Art said, "Antoine, the way you talk!"

Then suddenly they all burst out laughing, and this led to another group hug and some more cackling.

"Girl, just hand me that letter. As a matter of fact, it is blackmail. Mom embezzled some money many years ago. She paid it back, but these puke-heads from Cobleskill, this skanky bitch and her annoying husband, they're trying to get more money out of her since I got rich, and this letter has something to do with all that long-ago crapola. But don't tell anybody at Golden Gardens. Mom is over being a criminal — it was after Dad died and she was distraught — and nobody at the home has to worry about her filching anything."

Antoine shook his head and grinned. "Well, that Rita! Who would've thought. Did she do time?"

"No, the police don't know. That's how she got blackmailed."

Antoine produced an envelope from his back pocket. "I sat on it, so it's squished."

Hunny opened the envelope and laid the contents on the kitchen table. We all bent down and studied it. The letter itself was brief. It had been typed on a word processor, and it read:

Hello Rita,

Congratulations to your homosexual son for winning the Instant Warren lottery. I suppose he will now be able to indulge in many types of illicit activities that would turn the stomach of the average taxpayer.

However, we must now invoke the clause in your contract with us that triggers a higher compensatory award based on your family's ability to pay. We have demanded half a billion dollars from your son Huntington. If this amount is not paid by next Wednesday, we will go to the police. Also we will notify Golden Gardens and the Mount Zion Methodist Church.

Maybe you had better talk Huntington into coming to his senses and pay up. In return for your cooperation in this matter, we will return the original agreement to you and we will consider this unfortunate business, which has been so painful to all of us, closed.

Yours truly,

Your Disappointed Former Employers, A&C B — — — — .

Along with the letter were three photocopied pages of single-spaced typing in the form of a document. There were numbered items, lettered clauses, and subclauses with Roman numerals. The gist of it seemed to be, Rita Van Horn admitted stealing

$61,000 from Crafts-a-Palooza, and her restitution included interest payments and assorted fees and add-ons. The additional amounts were to be determined by a complex formula that was impossible for any of us to decipher. It looked like a contract for one of the adjustable-rate mortgages cooked up by the type of shyster lenders who had sent millions of people plunging into bankruptcy over the past year.

I said, "So you have never seen this agreement before?"

"No, but Miriam has a copy," Hunny said. "Lewis said it looked real, but they didn't want to show it to anybody to have it checked out. Miriam said it would be too embarrassing."

Antoine said, "To me, it looks like a pile of shit."

"I think it could be exactly that," I said. "Or semi-shit at best. I know a lawyer who can look it over and give us an opinion and keep his mouth shut. May I take this along? I'll have it copied."

"Maybe you shouldn't make any more copies," Hunny said. "What if it fell into the hands of FPAAC? Or Bill O'Malley?"

The phone rang again and Hunny sighed. "If this is another reporter, I'm turning them over to Marylou. She is my press representative, and she has been doing an excellent job."

Hunny picked up the phone and identified himself. And then almost immediately he went white.

"Yes, yes. Oh. Oh no! Yes? Oh. How much? Oh, all right, all right! Six thirty. Yes. I'll wait for you to call."

He hung up and said in a quavering voice, "They've got Mom. They want twenty thousand dollars for her. Oh God, oh God!"

Art said, "Twenty *thousand* dollars? Not twenty million?"

We all looked at Hunny. "That's what the man said."

CHAPTER ELEVEN

"They're calling back at six thirty," Hunny said, his voice thin and wobbly. "When they call, they'll give us instructions on where to leave the money. The guy said don't go to the police or they will torture Mom and kill her." Hunny buried his head in his hands and wept. "My God, my *gawwdd*!"

I tried to retrieve the caller's number but it was blocked. I said, "We don't know who this person is, so we can't deal with this on our own. Six thirty is under two hours. That's enough time to get the police to monitor and trace the next call. I think you should do that, Hunny. The alternative is to make your own arrangements for a swap — the money for your mom — and hope that these people can be trusted to keep their word, and then track them down after your mother's been returned. But that's risky, since we have no idea what kind of people the kidnappers are."

Art muttered, "Those bastards."

"Your mom is an old lady who had a good life," Antoine said. "But her time hasn't come yet. I just know it. I would just pay the twenty K. Girl, that's pocket change for you."

I said, "The caller was a man?"

"Yes. Or a serious dyke-a-rooney. But I think a man, yes."

"But it was not a voice you recognized?"

"No, I'd have recognized a voice I recognized. Oh, Lord, what am I saying? I think I need a drink. Artie, dear, can you fetch me the Jack Daniels?"

"Of course, luv."

Art retrieved a bottle from under the sink and said to Hunny, "Anyway, you don't have twenty thousand dollars in cash. How much do you think you have on hand?"

"Seventy or eighty dollars."

"I might have a hundred."

"I could come up with forty," Antoine said.

"I have the billion dollars in my checking account," Hunny said. "But my ATM limit is five hundred a day."

"Even if you went to forty different ATMs," Antoine said, "I don't think it works that way. I've tried it."

The phone rang again and Hunny grabbed the receiver.

"Huntington Van Horn speaking. No, no, I have not. Now, I am quite busy. Please speak to my press representative, Mrs. Whitney. I'll send her out in a few minutes, but right now she is helping the boys with their homework."

Hunny hung up and said, "It's that obnoxious woman from Focks News. She says Bill O'Malley wants to interview me tonight at the Focks studios in Albany, and do I have a lawyer yet, and when can I do a pre-interview? I told her to talk to Marylou. In fact, I think Bill O'Malley should interview Marylou instead. I've had my fifteen minutes of fame, and do you know what? I am *sick* of it. If I hadn't won the lottery, none of this with the Brienings and the blackmailers and the kidnappers would ever have happened! Oh, God, God, what should I do about Mom? Oh, poor, poor Mom. Donald, do you really think they would hurt an old lady like that? Oh, she must be so frightened."

"I don't know if they would actually harm your mother, Hunny. But because we know nothing really about who we're dealing with here, it's probably best to notify the police. The Albany cops have some competent people working for them these days, and they and the state police have the resources to put an operation together fast. They could trace the call when it comes in at six thirty, and they could monitor the cash pickup — and maybe even arrange for you to borrow the cash — and then track the kidnappers to wherever you mom is being held. The twenty thousand figure suggests to me that these people are small-bore amateurs who aren't likely to grasp what they're really into. This doesn't sound like the mob or some Mexican drug cartel or a major psychopath. What it sounds like is some opportunistic hapless dorks. These are the kinds of people cops run into all the time, and dealing with them is generally a piece of cake."

Hunny slugged back some of his whiskey and thought this over. "I guess you're right, Donald. Let the pros take over. I just have such bad memories of the Albany cops. In the seventies and eighties I had some unfortunate run-ins. For girls like us, they were the Gestapo."

"I remember. But nearly all of those goons are gone. I know somebody in the department I can call and get the ball rolling if you decide that's the way you want to go, and it's what I suggest. But you really have to decide now."

Hunny lit a fresh Marlboro from one that was half smoked. He seemed about to speak when the phone rang again.

"Hunny speaking." Now he looked irked. "Stu, I told you I would help you out, but I am too busy to take care of you just now. Yes, you will receive one thousand dollars, and yes it will be in cash. Detective Strachey will get the money to you this week. But I can't deal with that matter at this particular moment. Don't you know that my mother is missing from Golden Gardens?" Hunny listened and shook his head. "Are you calling from the Watering Hole? No wonder you're out of the loop. Now, call me early in the week and we'll make some arrangements. No, girl, I haven't forgotten all the nice times we had, but right now I have more pressing matters to worry about, and I am going to hang up. Good-bye, Stu."

"Stu Hood?" Art asked.

Hunny nodded.

Antoine said, "I have enjoyed Stu's company on a few occasions. Stu can be fun. Just so he doesn't ask you for a match."

I had my cell phone out and was poised to dial the number of a young Albany police detective I knew who was smart and competent and would not likely be freaked out by Hunny's entourage or his personal style.

But now Hunny's phone rang yet again.

"Hunny speaking." He stared hard at the receiver. "*What?*" He listened with big eyes. "Are you serious?" Now he was slumping over the table and shaking his head. "Did you call before? About ten minutes ago?" He looked exhausted, on the verge of collapse. "Well, someone *else* claims to have my mom also. Why should I believe you? What is *going on?*"

I leaned down with my head next to Hunny's so I could also hear the voice on the phone. Hunny was wearing some kind of heavy cologne, but his whiskey-and-cigarettes aura was even more potent, and he smelled like a figure from a long-ago era. I felt both revulsion and nostalgia.

I heard an unaccented man's voice, a bit gravelly, say that Mrs. Van Horn could not come to the phone because she was in the bathroom "taking a tinkle," but he could prove that he was holding her hostage. He said that she was wearing a bathrobe and slippers and she was a short, heavy-set lady with blue eyes and gray hair and her hair had recently been "done."

Hunny said, "That was on TV. Everybody in Albany County knows what Mom was wearing and what she looks like."

"If you want the old lady back in one piece," the voice said, "it's going to cost you ten thousand dollars. Put the money in a paper bag with *Mom* written on it and leave it on the bench outside Price Chopper on Delaware Avenue at seven o'clock. Then we will let her go. If you don't do like I say, I might have to get rough with your mother. Punch her in the face or somethin'."

Hunny looked at me, and I shook my head. He said, "I think you are full of it," and slammed the phone down.

Again, I tried to retrieve the caller's number, but this number was blocked, too.

"Was this another one?" Art said. "A second kidnapper?"

"He said I should leave ten thousand dollars on a bench outside the Delaware Avenue Price Chopper. He sounded like a complete doofus. Artie, girl, I think we're going to have to get an unlisted number. I'll call Verizon tomorrow. They'd be closed today, it being Sunday."

"This kidnapper was cheaper than the last one," Antoine said.

"If your mom wasn't in grave danger, you could almost shop around."

I said, "This one did sound like a flake. If he's somehow for real, he'll call back. It's possible the first call was also a hoax, but you shouldn't take that chance. I'm going to call the police, Hunny."

"Oh, yes, Donald, I suppose you must. Do whatever you think is best."

I made the call on my cell phone and luckily was able to reach my friend in the Albany PD. I explained the situation, and he said he would (a) notify the Rensselaer sheriff of this new development and (b) explain to the detectives on duty in Albany that they needed to set up a trap on Hunny's phone line, and then be prepared to surveil the ransom drop-off and follow the kidnappers to wherever Mrs. Van Horn was being held. I said I couldn't guarantee that this wasn't a hoax, but my contact agreed that we couldn't risk that the threat wasn't real. He said that kidnapping claims directed at the very wealthy always had to be taken seriously. He said two Albany PD detectives would arrive at Hunny's house within ten minutes.

Just as I was finishing up with the cop, there was a ruckus in the living room, and the kitchen door flew open. An excited Marylou Whitney came crashing into the room bathed in white light, which we soon saw was from the television lights mounted atop a video camera. She was trying unsuccessfully to keep a pinch-faced, scowling middle-aged man in a jacket and tie from entering the kitchen with her. The man looked at Hunny and barked, "Huntington Van Horn? I think you need to answer a few questions. This hoax has gone on long enough, and so has your refusal to return the billion dollars that came out of the pockets of hard-working Americans who do not support the radical homosexual agenda."

Antoine said, "Who is this Froot Loop?"

"Girl, I guess you don't watch Focks News," Hunny said. "I don't either, but I recognize Mr. Bill O'Malley from seeing his picture on *Inside Edition*. Come on in, girl, sit your skinny ass down here and I'll pour you a drink. Or would you prefer some weed?"

CHAPTER TWELVE

"Hunny, I don't think this is the right time for a television interview," I said. "The police will be here any minute now, and we have to deal with the urgent situation concerning your mom."

Beady-eyed and blotchy, O'Malley thrust a microphone at Hunny and barked, "We know this missing mom business is a hoax! We have our sources at All-Too-Real TV, and we know that you have been in touch with them about getting your own reality show. Do you deny it?"

Hunny blinked into the lights mounted on the camera that was aiming at him. "You know, Bill," he said, "you are a wee bit cuter in person than you are on TV. But I have to say, in the cutie-pie department you are a long, long way from competing with Missy Matt Lauer."

"Careful what you say, luv," Art said. "You know what happened last time. Nelson and Lawn might be tuning in."

"Anyway," Hunny said, "my people told your people in no uncertain terms that I would only talk to Anderson Cooper. Did your assistants not inform you?"

"That's right, Hunny," Marylou said, "I did make that abundantly clear to that Focks gorgon."

"Anderson Cooper's ratings are a tenth of what mine are," O'Malley snorted. "Now, you have not answered my question. I am going to ask it one more time. Have you or have you not been talking to All-Too-Real TV about a reality show deal? Just answer the question. Is your answer yes, or is it no?"

"I don't think you should talk to this liar," Antoine said. "Bill O'Malley called President Obama a communist."

"I never said any such thing. But he *is* a socialist, and he is destroying our country and robbing us of our precious freedoms. But right now taking my country back is beside the point. You still have not answered my question, Huntington. Are you in negotiations for a reality show on All-Too-Real? Keep in mind before you answer that anything you say can be held against you in the Focks News court of public opinion."

Marylou said, "Hunny, should I call security?"

Hunny looked at me, and I nodded, and Marylou turned in her ball gown and left the room.

I said, "O'Malley, go fuck yourself."

"Who are you, mister? Maybe you need to have your mouth washed out with soap."

Jane Trinkus said, "Should I leave that in? I can bleep it just enough to get it by the FCC, but viewers will know that you have been disrespected, Bill. It makes you look small, but it's great television."

Now another cameraman appeared in the doorway, and the young woman from Channel 13 who Timmy and I saw Wednesday night on TV at Hunny's won-the-lottery party edged into the kitchen in front of the videographer and said, "It seems unjust to the local media that out-of-town people should get an exclusive at this tragic time, Hunny. We really think out of fairness we need to be included."

"Tragic?" Hunny asked, going pale. "Has Mom's body been discovered?"

"No, I mean to say, tragic that she is still missing. She is, isn't she? Or have there been late-breaking developments?"

Waggling her fingers, Trinkus said, "Oh, there have been *developments*, all right. How do you spell H-O-A-X?"

O'Malley shook his head vehemently at Trinkus and mouthed *Our story*.

Now the two large Gray Security guys came in, and I said, "These media folks need to be led out of here. They are trespassing."

"Let's go," said the bigger of the two men.

"Who do you work for, Hugo Chavez?" O'Malley said to the

security man, who looked Hispanic but had given no indication that he might be Venezuelan.

Now O'Malley turned and looked directly into the Focks camera and intoned, "Obama's America. The America of Barack Hussein Obama is the America you are witnessing first-hand. *This* is what the United States of America has come to. The Founding Fathers must be weeping, and so, my friends, am I."

"Yeah, let's go," said the security guy. "Mr. Van Horn don't want you in here no more. Keep movin' out the door."

"Resist a little," Trinkus whispered. "Make him cuff you."

O'Malley shrugged that off and followed his crew and the Channel 13 team out of the kitchen, past a scowling Marylou Whitney and the twins, who had been hovering in the doorway holding their schoolbooks and passing a joint back and forth.

No sooner had the media departed than two burly guys in jackets and sport shirts strode into the kitchen. The older, larger, grayer of the two asked for Mr. Van Horn and introduced himself as Detective Lieutenant Card Sanders of the Albany Police Department. The smaller one was a Sergeant Lester Nechemias. Glancing uninterestedly past Art and Antoine, Sanders asked me if I was PI Strachey, and when I said I was he asked Hunny and me to tell him why we believed Hunny's mother had been kidnapped. Hunny described the first kidnapping claim that was phoned in. For the record, I added that there had been a second call from another claimant. I said the second call was almost certainly a hoax, but we couldn't be sure about the first one, and we had decided not to take a chance that it wasn't genuine.

Hunny said, "The first people said they would torture Mom and kill her, and the second ones said they would punch her in the face. She is so frail, and I'm afraid that even if they don't hit her or anything she might have a heart attack. So we have to rescue her as fast as possible. Oh God. Mom must be so *wrecked*."

"Does your mother have heart trouble? Is she on some kind of medication?" Sanders asked.

"Just Ativan once in a while. Mom would prefer bourbon, but

Golden Gardens keeps her on the straight and narrow in that regard."

"Mr. Van Horn, we'll do everything we can to get your mother back unharmed," Sanders said. "Verizon is set up, and when the kidnappers call back at six thirty we'll know within a minute or two where the call is originating. If it's a cell — and they may be smart enough to use one — the caller may be in motion and it will take longer to triangulate on the location. So what I'd recommend is that you make a plan to hand over the cash. What you want to do is, try to get the kidnappers to make a switch at a particular location, your mom for the money. But if they absolutely insist that the cash be dropped in one place and they say they'll release your mom someplace else, you'll just have to go along. APD is getting together a bag of twenty thousand dollars in marked bills and that bag should arrive here by six fifteen. You can repay APD the twenty K tomorrow at District Two after the banks open."

"Get my mom back in one piece," Hunny said, "and I'll give every officer involved a bonus of one million dollars."

Art screwed up his face and Antoine's jaw dropped.

Sanders said, "That's not at all necessary, Mr. Van Horn."

Sergeant Nechemias added, "Police officers are not permitted to accept gratuities from citizens, sir."

"I used to hate the Albany cops with a passion," Hunny said. "Back in the eighties, I got dragged into District Two seven times for giving blowjobs in the park, even though I wasn't harming a living soul."

The two detectives pursed their lips in apparent disapproval of the Albany police tactics of an earlier era but did not offer any present-day endorsement of public-park free love.

I said, "After Mr. Van Horn won the lottery, his being gay brought out a certain amount of right-wing hostility from individuals and from groups such as the Family Preservation Association of Albany. I take it you all are having a look at them, at least in connection with last night's shooting."

"At least," Sanders said, but didn't expand on that. He did add, "Don't worry. APD has plenty of experience in handling the weirdo types that celebrities can attract." Apparently the detective meant that Hunny's detractors were the weirdoes and Hunny was the celebrity, a nice attitudinal switch from two decades earlier that left Art, Antoine and Hunny looking satisfied.

The phone rang again. Hunny started, and then he stared at the thing with fright. Hunny's kitchen wall clock — with its picture of a naked Jack Wrangler and the clock's phallus-shaped big hand protruding from the one-time porn star's groin — showed that the time was just five fifty, forty minutes before the kidnappers said they would call back.

Sanders said, "Answer it. The call is being monitored." Sanders took out a cell phone. "I'll be able to listen in on this."

Hunny picked up the receiver and said, "Huntington Van Horn speaking." After a moment, he relaxed and said, "Nelson, yes, it's true. Apparently Mom has been kidnapped. But I can't talk now, 'cause we're waiting for the kidnappers to call back. We have call-waiting, but I don't want to get confused. I'm confused enough as it is." He listened some more. "Uh-huh. Yes, but I don't see why they're calling off the search just because of the kidnapping, which we don't even know for sure if it's real." More listening. Sanders was looking over at Nechemias and giving him just a hint of a family-tension-coming-to-the-fore eye roll.

"Oh, wait!" Hunny's eyes got big. "It's call-waiting. It might be the kidnappers calling early. Nelson, hang on." Hunny hit flash. "Huntington Van Horn speaking." He frowned. "Miriam, I just told Nelson, I *can't talk now*. Do I have to spell it out for you with a red crayon? I am waiting for the kidnappers to call back with instructions, and… No, I am not going to go on Matt Lauer again, and, no, I am not going to go on Regis and Kelly at all. Unless somehow it would help get Mom back. Then I would go on. Look, I have to hang up. I'm sorry. I'll talk to you when we know what on earth is going on with Mom and with — everything else."

Hunny hung up. "Oh, phooey! I just hung up on Nelson,

too. Well, he'll call back if it's important. Anyway, I don't even remember why he called."

"Probably about your mom," Antoine said. "Did Nelson say the sheriff is calling off the search?"

"Yes, the East Greenbush authorities got wind of the kidnapping, and also I suppose budget considerations are coming into play. Plus, it's suppertime, and Methodists like to eat. Oh Lord, I wonder if the kidnappers are feeding Mom. She likes to eat at five thirty sharp, and now it's past six."

The phone rang again, and Hunny stared up at it. Sanders nodded, and Hunny gingerly picked up the receiver. "Huntington Van Horn speaking. Oh, no, I'm sorry. No, I can't deal with that now. My mother is missing and I need to keep this line open." Hunny listened for a moment longer and then snapped, "I *said* I can't deal with that now. Didn't you hear me *say* that? Good-*bye.*"

Hunny hung up. "It was the Democratic Senatorial Campaign Fund. I sent them ten dollars once, and now they call every three days."

Art said, "You should tell them that if they call again at meal time you're going to give a billion dollars to the Republicans. Though they might think you're joking."

"No, in fact if they call back I am going to make a big donation to the Democrats. Maybe fifty million or something. Oh, Lord, Art, I guess I do have to be a little careful with my money. If I give everybody at BJ's a million — everybody except Dave DeCarlo, that is — and fifty million to the Democratic Senatorial Campaign Fund, and a thousand to Stu Hood, and a thousand to Mason Doebler, plus the flat-screen TVs at Golden Gardens, and then of course maybe half a billion to the Brienings, oh my God, I'm going to be down to my last couple of hundred million dollars. And then of course I promised the twins I'd put them through medical school, too. That's sure to cost an arm and a leg."

"Do you and Mr. Malanowski have children?" Sanders asked.

"Just our pool boys, Tyler and Schuyler. They attend HVCC and live with their parents in Schodack. But their home situation is less than ideal, so Artie and I do what we can to look after them."

Sanders said, "You mentioned someone you called the Brienings who might receive half a billion dollars. Are these relatives of yours?"

Hunny froze, and I could all but see the scenario unfolding inside his head: the Albany PD rescues Rita Van Horn from kidnappers and then notifies the Albany County DA, and Mom is immediately arrested for embezzlement.

Hunny said, "No, the Brienings are not relatives. Just good friends." He peered up at Sanders, probably looking for doubt or suspicion in his face. Sanders did look mildly puzzled, but before he could say anything, the phone rang again.

Hunny looked up at Jack Wrangler. "Oh boy. But what's going on? It's not quite time yet."

"Maybe they are unfashionably early," Art said. "Kidnappers don't have to be well-mannered."

Hunny picked up the receiver again. "Huntington Van Horn speaking... No! No, Jane, not now! Look, okay, yes, all right, I give in, I will talk to Bill, since it seems that Anderson Cooper is nowhere to be seen, and Bill did take the trouble to drive all the way up here from New York. But it will just have to wait until later tonight or until tomorrow. Right now I just need to get my mom back. But do not phone here again in the next hour, and in fact I have asked you once and I will ask you one more time, puh-leez deal with me through my press representative, Marylou Whitney... No, Jane that person in my living room most certainly *is* Marylou Whitney. It's the racing season at Saratoga, and Marylou is always up from Palm Beach for the month of August. In fact, the racing season just wouldn't be the racing season without Marylou jetting in, and sometimes she stays over for a few days with Artie and me. Now, dearie, I really do have to be off, so you just cool your jets, okay, girl?"

Trinkus must have said something else, but Hunny wrinkled his nose and hung up.

Antoine said, "Hunny, honey, I don't know why you even lower yourself to talk to those conservative medias. They just gonna fuck you over, girl, you better believe it."

"I know, dear one, that the only thing those folks are really up to is wrecking my last nerve. That's what they get off on. But I want to go on Focks anyway and try to win over a few listeners. I think if some people see how nice and well-adjusted and happy-as-a-clam I am, and Art and I am, that will be doing a good deed for gay America. Gay people all over the country will thank me for it, and it's just a responsibility I have to fulfill. It will help the cause of gay marriage and gay equality, so I must use this occasion to speak out."

This sounded as if it could lead to Lawn getting more complaints from his Dartmouth classmates. But before I could say anything to that effect, Jack Wrangler's member indicated that at last it was actually six thirty, and, on schedule, the phone rang once again.

CHAPTER THIRTEEN

"Oh, God, just don't hurt her," Hunny told the caller. "You can torture me if you want to, but my mom never hurt a flea, and she is just the sweetest old gal you'd ever want to run into — everybody says that about her — and I am begging you just to let her go as soon as I drop off the money."

Sanders was listening on his cell phone and nodding at Nechemias. Art, Antoine and I stood straining to hear any sound that leaked out from the receiver next to Hunny's sweating ear, but I could make out only an occasional hiss or low growl.

"Yes, yes," Hunny said. "I understand. No, no, I have not notified the police. Why would I do that?" He reached up and showed us his crossed fingers. "Twenty thousand dollars is nothing to me, and I will certainly pay you anything at all to get my dear mother safely back in my arms."

Sanders' eyebrows went up. Hunny seemed to be telling the kidnappers that they could have extracted a much larger sum from him, and perhaps they still might. But they did not up the ante, apparently, for Sanders began to nod again, and Hunny said, "I understand. I should put the twenty thousand…did you say in a gym bag? Oh God. I don't have a gym bag. I haven't set foot in a gym since seventh grade. Uh-huh. Uh-huh. Oh. Okay, a small suitcase. I have a small suitcase that is black with a purple ribbon on the handle so I can always spot it when the driver takes it out from the luggage compartment under the bus."

Sanders held his cell phone away from his face and whispered to Hunny, "Arrange for the swap."

Hunny said into the phone, "Just so Mom is right there when I give you the money, and we can be reunited at last. That's all I hope and pray for. To lay eyes on Mom. Then you can leave with the money."

Hunny listened again, and now he frowned. "Oh. But how do I know that you will do what you say after I drop off the money at TGI Friday's? Where will Mom be at that point in time? Yes. Yes. Uh-huh. Well, I guess I will just have to trust you." Sanders was nodding again. "But is Mom still in her bathrobe and slippers? If you drop her off at a store, she's going to be so embarrassed. Why not bring her to TGI Friday's and I'll get her right into my car and drive her over to Golden Gardens, and then we can all just forget this whole horrible episode?"

Sanders gave thumbs up to this suggestion, but the kidnappers must not have gone for it. Hunny looked glum again and said, "Okay, Mister Kidnapper, whoever you are. It will take me fifteen minutes or so to get out to Stuyvesant Plaza, depending on traffic. And I'll toss the black bag with the purple ribbon on the handle in the Dumpster behind TGI Friday's. Then I will drive out onto Western Avenue and head back this way. Before I get home, Mom will call this number and tell whoever answers the phone where she has been let off. Did I get that straight? Everything is all right, then?"

Antoine whispered, "Ask the asshole how you gonna get your suitcase back?"

Hunny shook his head and said to the caller, "I am paying you in order to save my mother, but I have to say to you that I am not sending you *any* of my thoughts and prayers. You really should be ashamed of yourself for scaring an old lady like this who is a good Christian and has spread good cheer wherever she goes." Sanders was energetically shaking his head at Hunny, who nonetheless added, "Don't let the twenty thou burn a hole in your pocket, ya shit-head."

Hunny hung up. "Should I have said those things? Oh Lord, me and my big mouth."

"They had it coming," Art said. "So, what's the situation? You're supposed to toss the money in a Dumpster at Stuyvesant Plaza?"

"Yeah, right now. I'm supposed to come alone."

Now Sanders was on his cell with somebody. He said to Hunny, "Get your black bag. The twenty K is in an unmarked

car out in front. Lester, why don't you bring that on in here?"
Nechemias hurried out the door.

"TGI Friday's will be covered by APD undercover officers. Just
take the money, Mr. Van Horn, and drive it out there and do like
the caller said. Do you know your way out there?"

"To Stuyvesant Plaza? Girl, of course I do."

"We still don't know where the caller was located — it was a
cell — but Verizon is working on that. We do know the number
of the cell and who the subscriber is. Does the name Elton
Steckenfinger mean anything to you?"

"Steckenfinger?"

"Yes."

"No. I'd remember that one. 'Ooo, I think my finger is
stecken. Just try to relax.'"

Sanders stared at Hunny. He must have been thinking that
celebrities are a species unto themselves, but in America we have
to love them no matter what.

Officer Nechemias came back into the kitchen carrying a
bulging paper sack.

Art said, "I'll fetch the suitcase, Hunny," and headed out the
door.

Sanders asked Hunny for his cell phone number and added
the number to his phone. He said, "I'll follow you, about a block
behind. Strachey, you ride along with me. Mr. Malanowski, you
should stay here with Officer Nechemias in case the kidnappers
call with the location of Mrs. Van Horn's drop-off. We will not
pick anybody up until Mrs. Van Horn has been rescued. But we
will surveil the Dumpster and tail whoever leaves with the money
bag."

Sanders suggested a particular route to the Stuyvesant Plaza
shopping center, and Hunny said, "Doll-face, that is how I would
go anyways. I grew up in Albany, sweetheart."

When Art arrived with the travel bag, Sanders stuffed the
stacks of hundred-dollar bills into it. He also retrieved from his

jacket pocket a small metal object with a Velcro back and inserted it into one of the bag's zippered side pockets.

"What's that?" Hunny said. "Some kind of explosive?"

"It's a small radio transmitter," Sanders said. "In case these bozos somehow get away from us."

"Oh, this is just like *The Bourne Supremacy*. Too bad Missy Matt Damon isn't here. Mom thinks Missy Matt is just *fab*-ulous, and what a thrill it would be for Mom if Matt Damon rescued her in person."

"Or even just his boyfriend," Antoine said. "What's-his-name."

"Is it Brad Pitt?" Art asked.

"No, he's straight," Hunny said. "Or so we are expected to believe."

"Now I remember, it's Ben Affleck," Antoine said. "I've heard that there is a video of those two going at it that is *hot*."

"Matt and Ben, or Matt and Brad?"

"Miss Matt and Miss Ben. But Lord, what a sandwich all *three* of those would make. *Ooo-eee*."

Sanders said, "You should be on your way, Mr. Van Horn. Do you feel up to doing this? Just keep in mind that I will not be far behind you. And I can also tell you that plain clothes officers are already positioning themselves out at Stuyvesant Plaza. We're going to make this work."

"Oh, it's only a matter of minutes then before Mom will be free. Praise de lawd! In fact, whoever picks her up, I think they should bring her over to the house here for a victory imbibulation. Artie, don't we still have some champagne in the fridge from the other night? Of course, Mumsie might go for something a little stronger, and let me tell you, so might I."

Hunny, in fact, had been sipping from a glass of amber fluid, and as he stood up he wobbled just a bit.

"Are you okay to drive?" Sanders asked, wondering perhaps if he was about to enable a DUI.

But Hunny slapped himself twice on his own cheeks and strode confidently toward the living room and the front door.

"Don't forget the ransom," Art said, handing Hunny the travel bag.

"Oh, heavens to Betsy, my mind is a sieve!"

We all followed Hunny through the living room and out the front door.

"Where are you off to, darling?" Marylou asked.

"I can't say," Hunny replied. "But our hugest problem is about to be solved. Then I guess I'll get busy solving the other ones. Girl, there is just no rest for the weary!"

"Will you be gone overnight?"

"I shan't think so, snookie-ookums. But if I don't return," Hunny added with a wink, "make sure the twins do their homework so they can get into Dartmouth and make Nelson and Lawn proud."

Marylou smiled agreeably, and we all moved down the front steps and toward the TV crews lined up on the sidewalk. They had their microphones poised, and Hunny turned and asked Schuyler and Tyler if he might borrow one of their T-shirts. Tyler whipped his off his well-formed frame and flung it to Hunny, who moved past the reporters and cameras with the shirt draped over his lowered head, as he cried out, "No pictures! No pictures!"

Hunny got into his old Ford Explorer with its all-but-treadless tires — the SUV's blue finish was grainy and dull but the tires were so shiny they looked waxed — and placed the travel bag with the money on the front seat next to him. Sanders' newer Ford sedan had been double-parked nearby, and he and I climbed into it.

As we followed Hunny down Moth Street, a couple of the TV people jumped into their vehicles and gave chase. But at the corner of Moth and Transformer, two APD patrol cars pulled into the intersection and cut off the press while Hunny sped up and moved on down the hill, with us not far behind.

I said, "If the First Amendment is suspended for thirty seconds, the republic will survive."

"Yeah," Sanders said, "Or thirty years wouldn't hurt either. Just kidding."

Sanders got on his cell phone and told somebody that we were on the way, and we should get to Stuyvesant Plaza at about six-fifty-five if traffic didn't bog down.

I said, "So who is this Elton Steckenfinger? Any idea?"

"Not yet. It's his cell phone, and it hasn't been reported stolen. Steckenfinger lives in Watervliet, and we've got officers on the way up there. They'll be cool till we see what happens at Stuyvesant."

"Does your experience suggest that these people will pick up the bag and then release Mrs. Van Horn?"

"I have very limited experience with abductions. But my training tells me that this thing has all the earmarks of dumb amateurs. The twenty thousand figure, for example. What's that about, for cryin' out loud? Why not a hundred thousand? Why not a million? These dickheads have to know that Mr. Van Horn won the Instant Warren. Half the people on the face of the earth have heard about Huntington Van Horn, the gay billionaire. And then there's the thing that whoever did the snatch is so confident that Mr. Van Horn wouldn't bring APD into it. Haven't these people ever been to the movies? The cops nearly always get called in the movies, and this is also true in reality. So, all the signs are, these are not well-organized geniuses we're dealing with here. They're dummies, I think, and the thing with dumb amateurs is, they're unpredictable. So, I really don't know what to expect, and we'll just have to see what we see."

We swung onto the interstate and headed west. We could see Hunny's Explorer two cars ahead of us. Hunny was doing fifty-five in the far right slow lane as the Sunday evening traffic roared by in the multiple lanes to our left. It was good that Hunny was dawdling, for he would need to exit I-90 at Route 85, and also in case one of his bald tires blew. The mid-August early evening sunlight was strong but shot through with the kind of tar-colored shadowyness that lets you know summer is not going to last forever and neither is anything else. Sanders had the windows up and the air conditioner on medium. Hunny had driven off with his car windows open — maybe because his Explorer's AC was shot, or because his was a cheaper model that had never had any.

Sanders gave our location to somebody on his phone — cops seemed to be exempt from the New York State prohibition against driving with a hand-held cell phone — and then he said to me, "Who are the Brienings?"

"Good friends of Hunny," I told him.

"I'll say."

"I'm not really sure who they are. Some people Hunny has a history with."

"He's giving them half a billion dollars? I find that mind-boggling."

"So do I. If I had half a billion dollars, I wouldn't know what to do with it. It's unreal."

"It just sounds weird."

"If you had a billion dollars, detective, what would you do with it? Where would you start?"

"Well, I wouldn't give half of it away the minute the check cleared, that's for sure. I'd buy a few people a beer, and then I would give the matter a whole lot of thought."

"Hunny Van Horn is impulsive. You must have picked that up."

"Impulsive." He laughed. "Well, he's an effeminate gay. They're a mystery to me. So, who knows? Are the Brienings also homosexuals?"

"Not that I know of."

"My supervisor's daughter is a dyke. She's hot, too. Two women. It's a turn-on. I saw her with her girlfriend and I thought,

Jesus, I wouldn't mind watching those two going at it. Or even getting in there. I wonder if my wife wouldn't consider that cheating."

"You could ask her."

Sanders followed Hunny down the exit ramp and onto Route 85 south.

"There are still guys in the department who badmouth gays. But not so much as before. You never know who you might be talking to."

"No. For heterosexual America, it's a minefield."

After a moment, Sanders said, "For example, I heard you were gay. So there you are. I wouldn't have suspected."

"No, I don't wear my bumper sticker on my forehead. But I do drive around with it on my car."

"Gays like Mr. Van Horn make a lot of people uncomfortable."

"This is true."

"If it wasn't for fruity guys like that, gay people would have an easier time. People get turned off, is what happens."

I said, "Ever hear of Stonewall?"

"Sure. The gays in the city revolted against the cops. Back in the sixties."

"Hunny Van Horn was there. Gore Vidal wasn't. And neither was I."

"Vidal the hairdresser?"

"No, he might have been there."

We were on Western Avenue now, Hunny about four cars ahead in the right lane. We passed the big State Office Campus, and we could see the entrance to the Stuyvesant Plaza shopping complex up ahead. Hunny signaled and turned into the access road, and then onto the sprawling tarmac, which was thick with the parked cars of Sunday shoppers and diners. TGI Friday's was close by, on the left, at the near end of a long strip of shops. Sanders parked within sight of the rear of the restaurant, and we watched Hunny halt next to the Dumpster near the restaurant's back door. Another Ford was parked about thirty feet from us, and I could make out a man and a woman seated in the front, their windows rolled up. I indicated this car, and Sanders said, "Ours."

Hunny got out of his suv, went around to the passenger side, and removed the travel bag from the front seat. He closed the car door, looked around until he spotted our car, then walked over to the Dumpster. The lid was closed on the Dumpster, and Hunny stood briefly taking in this apparently unexpected development. Then he lifted the heavy plastic top with one hand and held it open while he heaved the travel bag over the lip and into the receptacle. He let the lid fall back, glanced around, and walked back to his vehicle. No one in the area seemed to notice Hunny do this, or if they did they didn't react.

Hunny drove back out to Western Avenue and turned toward downtown Albany. We followed.

Sanders said to me, "We've got three teams of two monitoring the Dumpster. Now we wait for word from Sergeant Nechemias that the kidnappers have released Mrs. Van Horn and phoned the house with the drop-off information. But they'll pick up the ransom first, and we'll be told when that happens."

We were nearly all the way back to Hunny's house, heading up Moth Street, when Sanders received a call. He listened and said, "Okay."

"The bag has been picked up," Sanders told me. "By a man and a woman in an old Buick LeSabre. We're on them."

Back at the house, Hunny parked and again ran the gauntlet of mikes and cameras. We followed him into the house.

"No call yet?" Sanders asked Nechemias.

"Nothing. Just a few calls from media."

Hunny looked grim. "I *did* what they said. So, come on, you puke-heads, come on! Where is my *mom*?"

At eight o'clock, no call had been received from the

kidnappers. Sanders learned that the old Buick had been followed back to Elton Steckenfinger's second-floor apartment in a run-down section of Watervliet, and the man and woman who had taken the ransom bag had disappeared inside.

Hunny fretted — and drank — and nothing Art or Antoine said could console him. He refused to eat anything — the rest of us had some caviar and Ritz crackers left over from Wednesday's celebration — and Hunny's left hand developed a tremor.

Sanders talked to somebody on his phone just after eight fifteen, and a decision was made to confront and arrest the two people who had picked up Hunny's bag from the TGI Friday's Dumpster — presumably, though not necessarily, Elton Steckenfinger and a female accomplice.

Twenty minutes later, Sanders received a call. He listened and said, "Yeah, yeah. Okay. Yeah. Sure. That's all you can do. Okay."

Sanders rang off and said to Hunny, "I'm sorry to tell you, Mr. Van Horn, that your mother was not in the home of the people who took your twenty thousand dollars. In fact, my officers believe their story that they never held her captive at all. The Steckenfingers are a couple of crystal meth freaks who tried to exploit your situation. Everyone is extremely disappointed. As I'm sure you must be. At least we got the twenty K back."

Hunny choked back a sob. "But then, where is Mom? What happened to Mom?"

Sanders had no answer for that.

CHAPTER FOURTEEN

Bill O'Malley rarely left his New York City studio, but he had been driven up to Albany for what the promos on Focks News were calling a special investigation into "bombshell developments at the New York State Lottery." O'Malley had bumped Geraldo Rivera from his Sunday-night-at-ten spot so that he could score a scoop with his expose of "moral corruption involving underaged drinking, deviant sexuality, and impersonating a socialite" at the home of Huntington Van Horn, "the homosexual celebrity lottery billionaire."

Hunny had agreed to appear on the show, hoping that he could spread the news of his mother's disappearance to more people. Mrs. Van Horn still had not reappeared by nine thirty, and the East Greenbush sheriff had organized more volunteer groups to comb the area near Golden Gardens beginning at first light. An Amber Alert had been issued by the State Police. While Rita Van Horn was not a missing child, Hunny's celebrity afforded him the clout to bend the Amber Alert law to include the elderly. Meanwhile, Albany police had reported their arrest in the kidnapping hoax, and Elton and Marcie Steckenfinger had already been filmed doing a perp walk at Division Two headquarters.

I had driven over to the house on Crow Street to pick up some clothes and toiletries so that I could spend the night at Hunny and Art's, and Timmy and I settled in to watch the Bill O'Malley show together.

Timmy said, "Poor Hunny. I suppose this television appearance will be a lot different from his *Today Show* fiasco. His mother's going missing must be a sobering experience for him."

"Sobering? Not exactly that, no."

"Oh?"

"I advised him against doing the O'Malley show. He'd had more than a few shots of what I think was undiluted Jack Daniels and was semi-fuddled when he left the house for Channel 23. Anyway, the interview is sure to be unfriendly, and these promos we've seen can only begin to hint at just how hostile and unfair O'Malley is bound to be. But Hunny was determined to do it so that Mrs. Van Horn's picture could be seen by Focks News's millions of viewers. Hunny himself would prefer a cozy tête-à-tête with Anderson Cooper, but — media-savvy celeb that he's become — Hunny knows where the ratings advantage lies."

"I have to say, I really do feel sorry for the guy. Obnoxious as he often acts, it's apparent that Hunny is basically a good-hearted man who doesn't deserve all this hideous trouble that's come crashing down on him since he won the Instant Warren. And he must feel horribly guilty about his old mom being victimized, too. If, that is, her disappearance has anything to do with his own weird situation. Do you think it does?"

"Probably. Her life at Golden Gardens was apparently calm and uneventful until the state dropped a billion big ones in Hunny's lap. And the Brienings turning up, post-Instant Warren, might also have set something off with Mrs. Van Horn. Panicked her into doing — I don't know what."

"The news at six said Hunny was a well-liked and generous worker out at BJ's. Apparently he's giving his former coworkers each a million dollars. The manager of BJ's was interviewed and said he was concerned about a lot of associates — that new euphemism for retail wage slaves — giving notice first thing Monday morning."

"Yeah, something like thirty or forty people are going to receive a million each. Though Hunny is leaving out the guy who's suing him for half a billion. Dave DeCarlo must be having second thoughts. Oops."

"Channel 10 said Hunny was also planning on putting two young people through Dartmouth Medical School. That's pretty decent of him."

"Yes, Hunny is apparently concerned about a looming national shortage of podiatrists."

"Good for him. Podiatrists?"

It was ten o'clock, and I turned up the sound on the kitchen TV. Timmy was on a stool enjoying a late-evening snack of raisin bran with skim milk, and I had made a pot of strong coffee for myself.

A lurid BREAKING NEWS graphic flashed on the screen, and then the trumpet-accompanied announcement of a Bill O'Malley SPECIAL REPORT. O'Malley soon appeared, American flags flapping electronically to his right and left.

"Good evening, my fellow Americans…"

Timmy said, "My fellow Americans? What is he, the president? Good grief."

"Welcome to my special investigative report on corruption at the New York State Lottery." Staring gimlet-eyed into the camera, O'Malley fulminated for several minutes on the immorality and illegality of the Lottery Commission's refusal to withhold winnings from a man O'Malley said was not eligible to win the billion-dollar Instant Warren because of the poor example he was setting for America's youth. A state-run program, O'Malley said, should not be in the business of rewarding same-sex unions like that of Hunny Van Horn and his friend — O'Malley's fingers waggled a set of quotation marks when he said *friend* — Art Malanowski. Looking especially sanctimonious now, O'Malley said he certainly endorsed "tolerance for homosexuals," and he did not support crushing them with stone walls, "as is done in many Muslim countries." Up came some blurry video of a bulldozer shoving a stone wall over on two men in Arab garb who were lying prone in the sand and tied up and blindfolded. "However," O'Malley went on, "government tolerance is one thing and government participation in the radical homosexual agenda is not something any good American is willing to put up with."

"I wonder," Timmy said, "if O'Malley thinks the DMV is advancing gay rights by issuing us driver's licenses. God."

"Shh."

It was hard to imagine Hunny sticking around the Focks News studio and participating in this looniness, and in fact when O'Malley introduced an interviewee it was not Hunny at all, but the head of the Family Preservation Association of Albany County. The Reverend Payton Kalafut was a bulbous middle-aged gentleman leaning so far back in his chair that he seemed almost to be reclining and being viewed from above, as in a Busby Berkeley from-the-rafters shot. Looking up, he endorsed O'Malley's plea for tolerance by saying bulldozing homosexuals was "going too far." The reverend then argued nonetheless that "the dollars of tax-paying Christians must never be used to support immorality."

Timmy said, "Taxes don't support the lottery. Gamblers do. Most of them Christians, I'd be willing to wager."

"You should write O'Malley and demand a correction."

"I might."

Reverend Kalafut went on about suing the Lottery Commission, and gave a post office box where viewers could send donations to help cover FPAAC's legal expenses. Throughout the interview, O'Malley nodded sympathetically. He then thanked the reverend for "standing up for American family values" and wished him good luck with his lawsuit, which was "the Lord's own work." O'Malley told viewers he would be back after a commercial break, and then an ad came on for erectile dysfunction pills.

"At least," Timmy said, "by agreeing to participate in this horror show Hunny is going to come across as both brave and sympathetic. And maybe it will even help get his mom back."

"Let's hope that's the way it goes."

After a minute and a half, O'Malley reappeared, Old Glory waving next to each of his ears, and introduced Hunny, who was seated in the chair previously occupied by Reverend Kalafut. Slouching in his seat in an ill-fitting jacket and some kind of hand-painted necktie, Hunny looked wan, bleary-eyed and jittery.

"Huntington Van Horn," O'Malley intoned, "is the first winner of the New York State Lottery's Instant Warren drawing. Mr. Van Horn took home a check for a staggering one billion dollars last Friday when he appeared on another network to collect his huge check. Not content to simply say how fortunate he was, however, Mr. Van Horn, an advocate for gay rights, so-called, accepted his winnings and then made a suggestive comment about the male host's anatomy. That was an early tip-off that the New York Lottery Commission had made a tragic mistake, a mistake this taxpayer funded state agency has yet to rectify."

Hunny shot O'Malley a look that was both angry and injured and said, "This was supposed to be about getting my mom back. That…that Trinkus woman who works for you said…Trinkus said I could announce that Mom was missing from her nursing home and you'd put her picture on TV. So anyway, who cares about Matt Lauer's basket?" Hunny's diction was sloppy — the Jack Daniels had crept up on him — and as he spoke he squirmed in his chair like a child who needed to go to the lavatory.

"Yes, we'll get to the so-called disappearance," O'Malley said, arching an eyebrow at the Matt Lauer reference but otherwise charging by it. "Mr. Van Horn's mother has perhaps been misplaced by the Golden Gardens home for the elderly in East Greenbush, New York, an institution that state nursing home regulators need to take a close look at. I'll be doing an investigation of state regulators and their failings at a later date. There is also a good possibility that your mother's disappearance, so-called, could be a hoax connected to your own desire to obtain a contract for your own reality show on All-Too-Real TV. But right now, Mr. Van Horn, I have another photograph that I'd like you and viewers to take a close look at. Just look over there at the monitor."

Hunny flared, squirmed some more and was about to speak, but something caught his attention off to the side, and on our home screen up came a photo of a woman I took to be the actual Marylou Whitney. "Do you recognize this woman?" O'Malley demanded to know.

"Well, of course I do," Hunny muttered. "That is Mary

Cheney, the lesbian daughter of the former vice president and notorious war criminal Dick Cheney."

"Absolutely incorrect," we heard O'Malley say. Then the picture changed to the Marylou Whitney who was Hunny's pal. "And do you recognize this person, Mr. Van Horn?"

"That rectal vision," Hunny said in a W.C. Fields voice, "oh, I mean *regal* vision, is Mrs. Marylou Whitney, the horse fancier and gracious lady of Saratoga and Palm Beach. I rectalize…realize… reck-a-nize Mrs. Whitney because she is a very dear friend of mine. Marylou was telling me just this afternoon how happy she is that now I am even richer than she is. Isn't that a hoot? How d'ya like them apples, Bill O'Malley?" Hunny held his hand up and burped into it.

"Our show has evidence," O'Malley declared, "that the so-called lady shown on viewers' screens is in fact a female impersonator — a drag queen, if you will, who is just one of the retinue of gay lowlifes regularly harbored by you at your Moth Street home here in New York's state capital. These are people who will not only benefit directly or indirectly from the state's billion-dollar payout but will also, through becoming celebrities, influence young people across America to adopt the homosexual lifestyle. What say you to that?"

The camera went in for a close-up on Hunny, and it was now apparent that the hand-painted necktie he was wearing displayed the from-the-waist-up shirtless image of late porn star Jack Wrangler. Hunny scowled back at O'Malley and stammered, "What a…what a pack of bald-headed lies! I know that my friend is the real Marylou Whitney because I have seen the horse's face tattoo on her upper thigh just to the right of her ample bush. And if she did have a dick, *I* certainly didn't notice it. Or, if I did take note, and since then it has slipped my mind, I probably figured if Marylou Whitney wanted to have a dick sticking down from between her legs, then *that was her own freakin' business,* and it is certainly none of my business or yours!"

Now the camera cut to O'Malley's ashen face, as he said, "I apologize for that. We'll take a break and be right back."

Timmy said, "Yuck."

"I was a little afraid of this."

"This is not going to help. Not Hunny, not his mother, not any of the rest of us. Oh, Jesus."

Now another erectile dysfunction ad was running. The male in the couple was looking as if he himself had won the Instant Warren, and the woman we were supposed to assume was his wedded wife bore the expression of expectant awe you might find on a discount store greeting card rendering of the Annunciation.

I said, "I should not have let this happen. Hunny was set up. O'Malley and his people used Hunny's emotional state over his mother to lure him on and then provoke him and make him act in a way that confirms every Focks viewer's ugliest stereotype of gay men."

"Well, you said you advised him against going on. Maybe you should have hit him over the head with a chair."

"He was determined to do it. And he never even got to show the picture of his mother."

"O'Malley said her disappearance might be a hoax. Is that possible?"

"No. Who would benefit?"

"Maybe she staged it herself. Without Hunny's knowledge. To throw the Brienings off track. She has a history of deception, after all."

"The embezzlement?"

"Don, she's a criminal, for God's sake."

"Reformed. Mother Van Horn has been law-abiding in recent years. And sober."

The get-an-erection commercial ended, and O'Malley reappeared. His look was one of disgust mixed with triumph. The chair next to him was empty. He peered into the camera and said gravely, "As for the wisdom of the Lottery Commission awarding one billion dollars to a plainly unstable radical homosexual who is going to utilize his celebrity to promote sexual deviance and poor taste, ladies and gentlemen, I rest my case."

O'Malley glanced to his right as a noisy commotion broke out, and soon we could hear a plaintive cry. "Mom! *Mmmmooooommm!*"

"We have plenty more evidence," O'Malley went on, trying to ignore the ruckus, "that Mr. Van Horn is morally unfit to receive a large sum from a state agency. Focks News has learned that a former altar boy was served alcohol by Mr. Van Horn and sexually violated by him when the boy was a minor."

I said, "Oh no. Stu Hood!"

"The arsonist?"

But the picture that came on the screen was not Hood but that of Mason Doebler, the bearish owner of the Pontiac Firebird Hunny had been instrumental in wrecking.

Timmy said, "That guy was an altar boy?"

"Now a grown man," O'Malley said ominously, "but haunted by the pain and humiliation he suffered at the hands of the predatory Huntington Van Horn, Mr. Mason Doebler has informed Focks News that he is suing Mr. Van Horn for three hundred and seventy-five million dollars —"

More loud voices could be heard, and then suddenly Hunny appeared along with two women, one of them Jane Trinkus in her too-tight jeans. Trinkus had Hunny by the arm and the other woman was wrapped around his right leg, and they were trying to drag him away from O'Malley.

Trinkus screamed, "Stay live, stay live! America needs to see this! He's a terrorist!"

"Violence follows Huntington Van Horn wherever he goes," O'Malley boomed. "Late last night, supporters of Mr. Van Horn shot a Focks News cameraman who presently lies wounded in an Albany hospital. I urge you to offer your thoughts and prayers for…this brave cameraman."

The wrestling match proceeded a few feet from O'Malley, who leaned back in his seat and gawked.

"This is my mom!" Hunny moaned, and was trying to hold up to the camera a photo of a plump smiling old lady in a leisure suit and a fresh perm. "This woman is missing from Golden Gardens in East Greenbush, and she may be injured or abducted or lost and hungry!"

"None of that has been proven," O'Malley said, "although of course our thoughts and prayers also go out to this elderly senior citizen, whatever she might be up to."

"If you see her," Hunny gasped out, "please notify your local police department. And Mom, Mom, if you are tuning in, and you are being held against your will, or if you are hurt, I just want you to know that *I love you, Mom!* I love you, I love you, I love you! And if this has anything to do with the Brienings, don't worry, we will take care of everything. Don't worry, don't worry, don't worry, Mom! Just come home, Mommy! Mommy, just come home!" Hunny began to weep as the two women now dragged him out of camera range.

Bill O'Malley said, "Who are the Brienings?"

Chapter Fifteen

I drove over to Moth Street in time for Hunny's return from the Focks studios, a homecoming that was bound to be sad and awkward. I had already had a call from Nelson, who blamed me for what happened on the O'Malley show. Nelson claimed erroneously that it had been my job to keep Hunny out of any kind of trouble. In fact, I had been hired to deal with local thugs who turned up to harass or injure Hunny in one way or another, but not right-wing media thugs from Focks News. Still, I wondered if there was any way I could have kept Hunny from looking spectacularly foolish once again. Now I was even more determined to help keep Hunny from acting like his own worst enemy and — although I hadn't gone to Dartmouth and was not so much revolted by Hunny as fascinated by him — help keep him from becoming the cultural right's poster boy for abominable homosexual depravity.

Bill O'Malley had not gotten an answer to his question about who the Brienings were, and as I drove I tried to formulate a story for Hunny to use in case the question came up again. Hunny had been seriously drunk on the O'Malley show, so maybe he could get away with saying he had misspoken. And instead of the Brienings he had meant to say the Grindings or the Rhinestones or the Bite-sizes, not that those made any sense to anybody, either. But Hunny had a knack for brazening things out, so I supposed he could redeploy his broad range of improvisational talents.

While I had Nelson on the line, I told him I had met the Brienings, and it was my belief that they were not directly responsible for the disappearance, but that the threatening letter they had sent Mrs. Van Horn might somehow have caused Mother Van Horn to panic and bolt. Meanwhile, I suggested, we ought to respond with vague evasions to any questions from the press or the police about the mysterious Brienings.

The Mason Doebler threat was going to be harder to finesse. Doebler had apparently contacted O'Malley's people and lied about having been molested by Hunny, borrowing and whimsically altering Stu Hood's story, in a desperate attempt to extract more than the thousand dollars Hunny had promised Mason for his new catalytic converter. Three hundred seventy-five million dollars could put a real dent in Hunny's bank account. Hood was sure to get wind of this development, and perhaps he would then sue Doebler for either invasion of privacy or plagiarism. Either way, I knew of lawyers the aging arsonist could hire who would gleefully take this on.

I arrived at Hunny's house and parked across the street just as Art drove up and eased their dingy Explorer into the driveway, which was so tiny the SUV stuck out about a foot onto the cracked sidewalk. Several TV crews were still on the scene, but instead of pouncing in their normal way they approached the vehicle tentatively. As I approached, Art told them, "Mr. Van Horn is under the weather and will have nothing more to say to the media until further notice." The reporters all seemed to accept this. Some looked chastened, others bordering on queasy. They had either seen or heard about the O'Malley fiasco. The two Gray Security guards also stood off to the side looking pensive.

Hunny climbed out of the back seat with a Budweiser beach towel over his head and face, and Art led him as quickly as Hunny's unsteady gait would allow up the front steps and into the house. I followed close behind.

Antoine and the twins had left for the night, but Marylou was in the living room stretched out on the couch, her ball gown up around her knees. As we came in, Marylou switched off the TV, stood up and straightened her skirts. "Huntington, you naughty boy!" she said gaily. "Am I going to have to send you to the woodshed? Oh, my word, when they showed that female impersonator pretending to be me, and you said, no, that's not Marylou Whitney, that's Mary Cheney, the lesbian daughter of Dick Cheney, the war criminal, I just thought I was going to wet my pants!"

Hunny flopped into a chair and lit a Marlboro from a pack on the coffee table. "Well, they can insult me, Marylou. I am just one of Sarah Palin's reg-ler Amur-kins. But when they start in on the elite such as yourself, then they have gone too far. I have the deepest respect for the elite, especially an elegant society lady like yourself. Oh, Artie, dearest, I think I need a pick-me-up. Would you be so kind as to indulge your favorite old tosspot?"

Marylou tsk-tsked Hunny. "Is that wise, Huntington?"

Art's thinking was similar. "Hunny, honey, I'm shutting you off, and you are going right straight to bed. You have to be up bright and early when they resume the search for your mom. Or maybe she'll turn up while you're dreaming, and you ought to be bright and perky to welcome her back at the crack of dawn."

Hunny was suddenly alert. "The crack of who? The crack of Don Johnson?"

"How about Donnie Osmand?"

"Yecchh."

"Or Don Giovanni," Marylou said, and then trilled something Timmy would have recognized.

"How about Don Strachey's adorable crack?" Hunny cooed in my direction. "Donald, you aren't saying much. I think you have turned morose again. I can't imagine why. I don't suppose you caught me on the Bill O'Malley show, did you, by chance?"

"I did. Hunny, you might need to sober up until your multiplicity of problems have been taken care of. It would be really helpful if you did that."

"Artie, do get me one more shot, would you, please, doll face?"

"Nuh-uh. You've had more than enough. Donald is correct."

Hunny snapped, "All right, then don't! Anyhoo," he went on, his head suddenly pitching forward, "maybe we should all call it a night. Don, will you be joining Arthur and me in our bed chamber? If you do, you'll be glad you did. Ecstatic, in fact. Thrilled to your receding hairline."

"No, thank you."

"Oh, you must have attended the church up the street from the one I went to. Methodists sometimes allow a bit of leeway, but Presbyterians are generally stick-in-the-muds when it comes to sharing the masculine booty. Are you Presbyterian, Donald?"

"I once was. You nailed me, Hunny. Now I am more of an anarcho-vaguely Buddhist-secular humanist-worshiper of a good night's sleep."

Hunny arched an eyebrow and was about to say something else when his head suddenly toppled over again and his eyes blinked shut.

"Not to worry," Art told me. "Hunny isn't dead. He's just through for the night." Hunny's Marlboro dangled from his fingers and Art bent down and took it away. "Anybody want the rest of this? I hate to waste cigarettes. Do you know how much these things cost nowadays? I've tried to get Hunny to quit, mostly because of the incredible expense. But he said he'd give up food first, or his blood pressure pills, which cost nine hundred fifty-eight dollars a month, and his co-pay is almost two fifty. Of course, now that he's richer than Prince Harry, Hunny won't have to worry about co-pays and what have you. Still, where I grew up in Schenectady, you didn't waste money and put out a perfectly good cigarette until it was smoked down to the filter. Or if it didn't have a filter, my dad might get out the tweezers like it was a roach. Not that he ever knew what a doobie was. Anybody want this?"

"Just snip off the hot end and save the rest for later," Marylou said. "I've seen people do that in Palm Beach since Madoff."

I asked Marylou, "Were there any useful phone calls while Hunny was out? Nothing new from Golden Gardens, I take it."

"No, darling, there was just a brief call from Detective Sanders. He saw Hunny on Bill O'Malley, and he asked me if I knew who the Brienings were. Who are they, anyway? As Hunny's media representative, I need to be kept in the loop and on top of the information flow. And don't worry yourselves over what I might have to say to anyone on the subject of the Brienings, whoever they are. Everybody who knows me knows that spin is my forte."

Art said, "Hunny will brief you in the a.m., Marylou. The Brienings may actually be the biggest fly in the ointment we're having to deal with."

"No other calls?" I asked.

"No. Oh, there was one, actually. Do either of you know a Quentin Shoemaker?"

Art said no, but I said I thought the name sounded vaguely familiar.

"Mr. Shoemaker said he saw Hunny on Bill O'Malley and he wants to come down from Vermont where he lives and help Hunny out. He is one of the original Radical Fairies, he said. And now Mr. Shoemaker is part of a commune up in Ferrisburg called the RDQ, and he thinks Hunny is getting a raw deal both from horrid right wingers like Bill O'Malley and also from all the gay people in Albany and across the nation who are not coming to Hunny's defense as he gets dragged through the slime."

"That's where I heard of Shoemaker," I said. "I've read about the RDQ. It's a kind of neo-hippie group, the Radical Drama Queens."

"Oh, lovely, lovely! I think this is just the pick-me-up that Hunny needs at this point. I'm sure the RDQ will bring a breath of sanity and fresh air into all our lives. And at this dark moment, we certainly could use a ray of sunshine or six. Since Hunny won the Instant Warren, his life has just gotten so...*complicated.* Perhaps some people who have been placed on this earth to promote peace and love will simplify things and remind every one of us what is really important in life."

Art said, "Marylou, honey, what you are saying sounds an awful lot like wishful thinking."

That sounded right to me.

CHAPTER SIXTEEN

First thing in the morning, Hunny announced he was going to have "a shot of the twink that bit me," but Art said, "No, pootykins, I am shutting you the hell off again."

"Then bacon and eggs, it is!" Hunny declared heartily. "There will be plenty of time when I enjoy my customary elevenses to march into General Jack Daniels' office and salute smartly."

Hunny had phoned Nelson at the East Greenbush sheriff's office, where the search for Mrs. Van Horn had resumed, but no sign of her had yet been found.

Now the kitchen phone rang, and Hunny started and looked frightened. "Maybe this is about Mom. Oh Lord, oh Lord."

He picked up the receiver. "Van Horn residence." He listened for a minute or so with a look of consternation and finally said, "Well, maybe *you* should be in rehab — *butting-in rehab* is what you really ought to sign up for!" He banged down the receiver.

"It was just one of my thousands of non-fans," Hunny said glumly. "Somebody who saw me on Bill O'Malley. You know, boys, that entire portion of last evening is hazy. Tell me the truth. Was I charming, and was I an effective spokesperson for the celebrity community? Or did I arrive at the studio snockered, and did I hop around on one foot and stick my other foot up my ass so that it was coming out of my throat and looked really weird on TV and grossed everybody out?"

"The latter," I said.

"Donald," Hunny said, fumbling with a fresh pack of Marlboros, "how did you sleep? Were you comfortable enough on the guest room fold-out?"

"The metal bar in the middle hit me in the back. But I folded up the bed and placed the mattress on the floor and slept there. It was fine."

"On the floor! Donald, you are such a primitive. It's Jungle

Jim. It's Bomba the Jungle Boy. This is starting to turn me on."

Busy getting breakfast together, Art looked over his shoulder and said, "How do you like your eggs, Donald?"

"Scrambled, thank you."

The phone rang again. "Van Horn residence. Oh, Detective Sanders. I am so glad to hear your official-sounding voice. Uh-huh. Uh-huh. Yes, Detective Strachey is just to my port side. In fact, I was just about to offer him a glass of port. Here, let me put him on." To me, Hunny said, "Colonel Sanders says there is no news on his end, but he wishes to speak with you."

"I've been in touch with the East Greenbush sheriff," Sanders told me, "and people over there have resumed the search for Mrs. Van Horn. But they're starting to run out of territory the old lady might have wandered into on her own. It's looking more and more as if she got a ride somewhere, and yet nobody has reported picking up an elderly woman in her bathrobe and slippers. That pretty much leaves us with, she's with somebody she knows. Her family and friends all deny taking her anywhere, but there may be somebody who's been left out of that equation that you all are not thinking of. Would you please ask Mr. Van Horn about friends of his mother who maybe haven't been contacted yet?"

"Sure. Mr. Van Horn's mind is functioning more efficiently than it was yesterday, and I'll see what I can find out." Hunny looked at me cross-eyed and smacked himself on the forehead a couple of times.

"I take it," Sanders said, "that there have been no more calls from supposed kidnappers."

"No."

"An abduction is unlikely then. Anybody doing it would likely have made their ransom demands by now. But I'm still intrigued by these people the Brienings. Mr. Van Horn mentioned them again last night on Bill O'Malley. He said that if his mom was watching she should not worry about the Brienings, that he would deal with them. These are the same Brienings, I take it, that Mr. Van Horn might give half a billion dollars to?"

"Probably. Are you sure he said Brienings on O'Malley? Some of his speech was indistinct."

"You heard it as clearly as I did, Strachey. I've replayed the video of the O'Malley show twice. Now, what gives here? Who are the Brienings, and where do they fit into the equation? Look, I am playing straight with you, and I expect you to play straight with me. Otherwise, well…I don't know. You'll find that I am not a policeman to be screwed around with."

"Lieutenant, let me get back to you on that. I do appreciate your interest and concern."

"I'll be back over to Mr. Van Horn's residence this afternoon. I'll expect to be clued in. Do you hear what I'm saying?"

"Fair enough."

I hung up and said to Hunny, "Sanders is interested in the Brienings. You mentioned them on O'Malley last night."

"I did? What in heaven's name did I say?"

"That your mom should not worry about them. That if they had something to do with her disappearance, you would deal with them."

"I said that on TV?"

"Uh-huh."

"Blabbety-blabbety-blabbety. That must have been me."

"Yes, Hunny. Blabbety-blabbety-blabbety."

He thought this over and then winced. "I may have to go on the wagon. I've done it before."

"That would help a lot."

"For Mom. Just until she is safely back."

"Hunny, it would do you good," Art said. "You could slim down, too, while you're at it." Art retrieved two slices of heavily browned Wonder Bread from the pop-up toaster and set them on a section of paper towel next to a jar of grape jelly.

"I was off the sauce for three days when Larry Tralongo

died," Hunny said. "Larry was our first friend to die of AIDS. I thought everything was going to be different from then on, and I might as well get used to it. But I never did get used to it, even though there were many more opportunities — too many opportunities — to do so. I came home after Larry's funeral that day and got lit. However, Donald, I'm just a social drinker, I want you to know. I never missed a day of work on account of the booze. Oh, Artie, what time is it? Lord, I cannot *believe* that I'm not out at the warehouse right this minute punching in my time card and planning out my day of trying to grope a few of the stock boys."

"Why don't you just pretend," Art said, "that this is a workday and you're not going to have your first cocktail until after work. Later on you can be as social as you please. Just as long as you don't have to go on TV again."

Hunny chuckled. "Did I really call the other Marylou Whitney Mary Cheney, the war criminal's daughter?"

"You did. We were all so proud of you. Marylou and Antoine were rolling around on the floor, they were laughing so hard. The twins thought it was a riot, too, even if they weren't sure who Mary Cheney was. Tyler asked if she was part of that old folk-song group."

"Bill O'Malley must have swallowed his tongue."

"He thinks he's the unperturbed type, but you could tell that your remark got to him."

"Mom would have loved it. She'd have been falling out of her wheelchair."

"It's good that you insisted on showing her picture. O'Malley was just going to blow her off. He just wanted to distort everything and make you look bad. And then showing Mason Doebler and saying you molested him. What a lot of BS that was."

Hunny set down his coffee mug. "Was Mason Doebler on, too? I don't remember that."

"The twins taped it." Art said to me, "The boys know how to work the VCR."

"Oh. Should I watch it?" Hunny asked.

"No. Don't."

"What did Mason have to say? That he crashed his car while I was sucking his dick? He likes to go around making a big deal of that dumb incident."

"He said you molested him when he was an altar boy. He's suing you for three hundred seventy-five million dollars."

Hunny resumed eating his breakfast. "Okay, as of this minute Mason Doebler is off…my…list. He goes into the Dave DeCarlo bin."

"Mason and several others. You had calls earlier this morning from people we know who said not very nice things about you. Not our friends, but people we know. People who saw you on Bill O'Malley. Or on Channel 13 the other night. Or on *The Today Show*."

"Don't tell me who. Not yet. Well, at least I got Mom's picture on TV. I can't believe that nobody has called with news of her. Why hasn't anybody spotted her somewhere? Unless she has had plastic surgery. But it's been too soon for that. And Medicare wouldn't cover a makeover. It's cosmetic."

I said, "Are you sure, Hunny, that there is no one in your family or in your mom's circle of friends who might have picked her up and given her a ride somewhere? Someone Nelson or the police haven't contacted yet."

"I gave them a list. I wracked my brain."

"Somebody phoned your mom fifteen minutes before she left the nursing home. Is there anybody you can think of who might feel free to phone her at seven forty-five in the morning? That's pretty early to call most people."

"I know. Though since Mom eschewed the bottle, she's been one to rise and shine with the rosy-fingered dawn. So it could have been anybody who knows her."

"Right. So perhaps there is someone she knows that you're not thinking of. A church friend or a work friend maybe."

Hunny pressed the sides of his head hard in an apparent attempt to stimulate thought.

After a moment, he said, "Arthur, I need a drink. One."

"No. That would be unwise, dear one."

"Well…Godfrey Daniels! Am I going to have to start sneaking down to the coal bin?"

The phone rang and Hunny picked it up. "Yeah? Who be you?" He listened and said, "Well, you're not much of a role model either, bothering people at nine in the morning and calling them…crappy names and crap like that. Are you speaking for all the gay people in America? I very much doubt that, you evil queen!"

He hung up and said, "Verizon must be open by now. Artie, we really do need to get an unlisted number. Today."

I said, "You should probably keep this number as long as people need to reach you about your mother. This is not the time to be going incommunicado, even if you have to put up with some cranks."

Hunny shoved his plate aside and reached for his Marlboros. In his desolation, he looked so unlike the euphoric Hunny that Timmy and I had seen on Channel 13 five days before that I wondered if he might ever recover from what had turned out to be a stroke of stupendously bad luck for him, winning a billion dollars.

The phone rang again, and this time it was not another gay person calling up to criticize Hunny for embarrassing the homosexuals of America. This call was from Nelson, who was now over at Golden Gardens. He said Mrs. Kerisiotis had asked him again who the Brienings were. They had phoned the nursing home and identified themselves as "business associates" of Rita Van Horn, and they said they might drop by late Wednesday with some information about her that the management of Golden Gardens would find interesting. They told Mrs. Kerisiotis to be sure to mention their call to Nelson and Hunny.

CHAPTER SEVENTEEN

As I drove out to Cobleskill, low clouds moved in and soon I turned on the wipers to deal with a light drizzle. Swoosh, two, three — swoosh, two, three. Nissan, the waltz king. Did windshield washers Argentine tango? The temperature was up in the eighties, even with the rain. So if somehow Rita Van Horn was stuck out of doors she would not likely suffer too much from exposure to the elements, provided she was found soon.

Except, it seemed more and more likely that Hunny's mom had not just wandered off but had been picked up by someone, perhaps whoever had phoned her fifteen minutes before she tottered out the front door at Golden Gardens. It didn't make sense that whoever drove Mrs. Van Horn away had anything to do with the Brienings. Their investment was in keeping her in a spot where social pressure and the threat of humiliation would underpin their extortion scam. But their recent implicitly threatening phone call to Golden Gardens suggested that they might hold to their Wednesday deadline, whether or not Mrs. Van Horn was back at the home, and I needed to talk to them and buy time if at all possible.

Cobleskill looked fresh in the benign light rain, although Crafts-a-Palooza, lightly patronized on a Monday morning and smelling of what I took to be New York Thruway-restroom-scented candles, gave off a less welcoming vibe.

"You know what this is?" Clyde said, pointing a metal object at me. "It's a glue gun, and believe me, I know how to use it." He yelled at a curtained-off area in the back of the store, "Arletta! Arletta, that goon working for Hunny Van Horn is back."

She came through the curtains wielding her own weapon, a Mike Huckabee-brand crown of thorns. The wreath was still in its plastic wrapper, so if she came at me with it I would not likely be injured.

"So," Arletta said, "did you bring Clyde and I a big fat check from Rita's drunken son?"

"Drunken?"

"Oh, don't think we didn't see him on Bill O'Malley last night making an ass of himself and of every one of his sorry ilk."

"Then you must know that Rita Van Horn is still missing. Hunny is so upset he can't deal with anything else right now. I'm sure you understand that. Put yourself in his place."

Clyde said, "Mr. O'Malley thinks this missing-Rita shenanigan is all a hoax. He has proof, he said."

"Did he? I just heard a lot of wild speculation based on nothing at all."

"It's all about some reality TV show," Arletta said. "I would no sooner believe anything any of the Van Horns told me than I would believe Barack Obama."

I said, "Hunny turned down the offer of a show on All-Too-Real TV. His entire life has turned into a reality TV show, and he doesn't like it."

This caught Clyde up short. "Why would he say no to that? Don't those people on those shows get paid a lot?"

"Since we're so important in Hunny's life right now," Arletta said, "and Rita's, also, maybe Clyde and I could be on the show, too. Of course, then it would have to come out that Rita is an embezzler. No, I can see why they would try to exclude us. Anyway, we'll have plenty of money when Hunny splits his lottery winnings with us. Which will be just a couple of days from now, won't it? What's your name again?"

"Don Strachey."

Clyde said, "But, Arletta, after we get the half a billion from Hunny, then we wouldn't have to mention the embezzlement on the TV show. That stuff would be all squared away. We could just be there as Rita's former employers. And as well-wishers."

She screwed up her face. "That's true."

I said, "Let me run this by Hunny and get back to you

later in the week. There is also the possibility of Oh Look! TV doing a biopic of Hunny. His winning the lottery, plus dramatic episodes from the first Gulf War and probably some stuff about vampires."

Clyde and Arletta perked up even more. Maybe they thought they could play the vampires.

Arletta said, "Just make sure Hunny pays us the half a billion by Wednesday. We need to put a deposit on space at Crossgates by the end of the week, and we'll need time for Hunny's check to clear."

"I'll see what I can do. You understand, of course, that at this point Hunny's first priority has to be getting his mother back in one piece. If you think about it, that will be in your best interests, also. If anything happened to Rita — if she were to suffer a fatal stroke or heart attack, say, or become a victim of foul play — I guess both of you would in that case have to accept the fact that you are royally fucked."

"Watch your language in the presence of my wife."

"Sorry."

"Well, what are the police doing, anyways?" Arletta asked. "Are they investigating the hoax theory? Bill O'Malley is a man who knows what he's talking about."

"I know that the police are following every lead they can. The East Greenbush sheriff is coordinating with the Albany Police Department. The State Police are on the case, and there's talk of bringing in the FBI."

"The Van Horns are getting the celebrity treatment," Arletta said, and sneered.

Clyde looked puzzled. "Why shouldn't they?"

"Just because he won the Instant Warren? He's a pervert and she's a thief. This is what we've come to!"

Now Clyde grasped what his wife was getting at. "More of the same," he said. "Just more of the same."

"Obama's America."

I said, "The threatening letter you sent to Mrs. Van Horn was found in her room. So we know she received it. Probably on Saturday, the day before she walked out of Golden Gardens and has not been seen since. It does seem possible that your ultimatum — Hunny pays you half a billion or Rita faces exposure and humiliation — might have triggered some desperate act by Mrs. Van Horn. If so, are you prepared to accept moral responsibility for that?"

"Desperate act, like what?" Arletta asked.

"We can only guess. I suppose she might try to kill herself. Or has already done it."

"Oh!" they both cried.

"I'm not saying this just to frighten you, but there is also the possibility that she might try to get rid of the two of you. She is known to be distraught, and it was probably your letter that pushed her over the edge. What is your security situation here and at your home?"

Arletta was aghast. "Do you mean shoot us or something?"

"There's a shotgun missing from the office of Mrs. Kerisiotis, the administrator at Golden Gardens. There is no evidence that Mrs. Van Horn took it. In fact, she has no history of violence. All I'm saying is, the two of you might want to kind of lay low for the time being. And don't do anything more to provoke Rita Van Horn or her son."

Clyde had gone pale below his A-1 hairdo, but now Arletta was looking suspicious. "It sounds to me, buster, as if you are threatening Clyde and I. Trying to spook us and make us back off. Well, if you are, you just might want to try some other tact. We are both stubborn, and when we are in the right we stand our ground. We have our principles, and they matter to us more than life itself."

It was all I could do to keep from wrenching Clyde's glue gun out of his hand and gluing his wife's mouth shut. But I knew that that wouldn't help in the long run. I said, "I'll report back to Hunny what your current position is — that you all will be in touch again later in the week to try to work something out. Meanwhile, you'll be giving Hunny some breathing room to deal with his missing mom, who we all hope hasn't done violence to herself or is perhaps somewhere planning to bring grievous harm to others."

Clyde still appeared shaky, but Arletta's look hardened even more. She said, "Behind this curtain is a lockbox containing Rita Van Horn's confession of a major felony. It is a confession that will put that dirty old embezzler behind bars where she belongs unless Hunny Van Horn makes good on his mother's theft by noon on Wednesday. I said not Thursday, but *Wednesday.* Ya got that?"

CHAPTER EIGHTEEN

Hunny and Art had driven across the Hudson to East Greenbush, where Hunny had gotten into a sniping match with Lawn over Hunny's Bill O'Malley public psychodrama. I learned this during a phone call from Nelson as I was driving back from Cobleskill. I told Nelson the Brienings seemed not to have had any direct connection with Mrs. Van Horn's disappearance but that they were going to be a continuing threat, and we needed to get Hunny's mom back as soon as we could so that she wouldn't still be missing if and when the Brienings went public with their wacky charges and demands. Nelson said there was still no sign of his grandma, and both the sheriff's department and the search volunteers were becoming increasingly frustrated.

I arrived back on Moth Street just as Art and Hunny were parking the Explorer, and now another vehicle pulled up in front of me and shuddered a few times before its driver shut the engine off. The driver's door of a tiny gray Fiat opened, and a small man climbed out. The old car had a dinged and grainy finish, like the one on Hunny and Art's Explorer, and the driver also looked as if he had some mileage on him.

"Yoo-hoo! Anybody home on Queer Street?"

The man waved at Hunny and Art, who peered back at him quizzically. Most of the TV crews had not yet arrived for their daily stake-out, but a lone cameraman peered over at the little man. The two bruisers from Gray Security, camped on the porch swing, also took in this strange new arrival, something else for them to think about.

The man was ectomorphic and gaunt. He was mostly hair from the neck up, frizzy and white. He wore sandals and knee-length cargo shorts, though oddly he also wore a button-down oxford-cloth dress shirt and a large necktie with an image on it that I was not yet able to make out.

The man crossed the street as the security guys watched him, and Hunny and Art squinted at him warily. I caught up just as the man reached the sidewalk and cheerily introduced himself as Quentin Shoemaker and said, "And I'll bet you boys are Hunny and Art, Albany's richest cocksuckers. Am I right? I can spot one a mile away." He beamed.

This is when Hunny noticed that the necktie Shoemaker was wearing was identical to the one Hunny had worn on the Bill O'Malley show, a hand-painted image of Jack Wrangler's head and naked torso.

"Hey, girl," Hunny said, "that's my tie! You stole my Jack Wrangler necktie, you rapscallion you! You know, I saw His Royal Highness Missy Jack Wrangler in the back room at the Mine Shaft in 1978. Even got to touch it briefly, although there was an awful lot of pushing and shoving in that block-long queue. Maybe you were there, Quentin, unless, of course, you hadn't even been born yet, ha ha ha."

"Oh, I missed all that urban cuddling and cooing, Hunny. I'm a country boy. I was in Oregon rolling around in the mud with the other mountain fairies. As for not being born yet, I've been born so many times I've completely lost count."

Art looked apprehensive. "So what are you? Born again?"

"Yes, again and again and again and again and again."

"But not a born-again Christian, if I'm not mistaken," Hunny said. "Most of them are not as enthusiastic about cocksucking as you seem to be. Unless I misunderstood your greeting and you actually disapprove of that ever-popular activity."

"No, in fact if all those senators arguing about health care and the public option and the trigger and so on would just take off their clothes and give pleasure instead of pain to one another, we'd have a single-payer system like Canada's in place in no time at all."

"Hey, you should write your congressman."

"I did. I got a nice note back, too, saying he would be considering all sides in the health care debate and he valued my input."

Hunny and Art had a good laugh, and they introduced me, and we all walked into the house. The rain had let up, and patches of blue sky were breaking through, good news for the volunteer searchers across the river.

"You're a private detective?" Shoemaker asked. "I never met a real one. I sense that you are not like many of the men in your line of work. You are freer."

"Apparently. At any rate, today I am comfortably in the company of two men who own Jack Wrangler neckties. That must mean something."

Hunny led us into the kitchen and said, "Art, just one. I would like just one itsy-bitsy snort."

"No."

"My mother is missing," Hunny told Shoemaker. "So we are all very stressed. Oh, I suppose you know that. Mrs. Whitney told me you called. That was so nice of you to take an interest."

"It sounded to me as if you could use a few queer friends. Some of us at the RDQ commune saw you on TV, and we all just stood up and cheered. I said, 'Boys, behold! Can our eyes be deceiving us? He's on TV, and he is an unassimilated gay man!' Generally the gay people who appear on television are so assimilationist they might as well be het."

Hunny and Art stared at Shoemaker. Hunny reached for a cigarette, then changed his mind and just fiddled with the ashtray.

Hunny said, "I'm glad *somebody* thought I was fun. An awful lot of people sure didn't. That's all I aim to be, Quentin — friendly and fun. What's the point taking everything so *seriously*? At least when you don't have to."

"Yes, grown-up activities are necessary to making the world go round — plowing the earth, harnessing the energy of the waters, milking the goats. But acting grown-up all the time is utterly soul-destroying, and I could see immediately that you were not a man who had anesthetized or even strangled his inner child."

Art said, "Hunny wouldn't do that."

"Gay spirit is being crushed at every turn in our society equally by small-souled straight people who can only stand us if we act just like them, and by gay people who've lost their connections to the great spirits of the earth and the universe that made us large and free."

"Hunny is definitely large and free," Art said.

"Well, I am honored to know you. Both of you."

"Thank you," Hunny said, glowing. "Thank you so much."

Again, Hunny reached for a cigarette but then thought better of it.

"So, your mom left the nursing home and she still hasn't been found?" Shoemaker asked.

"No, and it's been over twenty-four hours. We think she went off with somebody, but for the life of us we can't think who."

"What is her birth date?"

"January twenty-eighth. Why do you ask?"

"One of our members, Savion Davenport, can do her chart and see if we can get a handle on what lies ahead. What time of day was she born on January twenty-eighth?"

"I don't know the answer to that."

"She's never had her chart done before?"

"Well, just Medicare."

"Savion is highly intuitive, so he'll figure it out."

Art said, "So you live in Vermont? We were over there one time several years ago."

"In Ferrisburg, near the lake. Most of the back-to-the-earth folks who moved to Vermont from New York in the '60s have semi-assimilated. A lot have regular jobs, and I can't argue with that. Not everybody can afford to swim with the dolphins, or needs to. A lot are doing righteous work — teaching, medicine, traditional healing, energy work, what have you. However, Dennis Bower, who was one of the original radical faeries on the West Coast in '71 is now a deputy assistant secretary of defense.

We may have to levitate the Pentagon again, ha ha, and reclaim Dennis's spirit!"

"Are there porpoises in Lake Champlain?" Art asked.

Shoemaker chuckled. "Aren't there porpoises everywhere? The thing is, not everybody can see them. Or is willing to. The Native Americans near Ferrisburg tell stories of porpoise-like creatures filling the lake like carp in a farm pond before the coming of the white man."

Hunny said, "There was an Indian on the Van Horn side of the family, a Mohawk. My sister Miriam claims that's just a story, but my mom said Dad admitted that it was true. About a hundred years ago. Some kind of *Song of the Loon* type of situation, except the Indian must have been straight."

"That may help account for your free spirit, Hunny. And don't be too sure your ancestor was straight. He could well have been a *berdache.*"

"What's that?"

"Berdaches are Native Americans who are free of gender straitjackets."

"We saw an Indian drag queen one time at Foxwoods Casino," Art said. "But I guess you're talking about something historical."

"Not necessarily. Drag queens are very much in the berdache spirit. Like your friend Marylou Whitney. I could tell even just talking to her on the telephone that she was deeply real and she was deeply special."

Art said, "Yes, in Palm Beach Marylou is famous for being the most glamorous woman with a dick in South Florida."

Hunny gave Art a look. "That is not funny, Arthur. Marylou would not be amused. She is somewhat self-conscious about her penis."

"I didn't mean it to be funny. I was just stating a fact. Anyway, on Bill O'Malley you defended Marylou's right to have a dick if she wanted to. You practically said it was in the Bill of Rights. So don't tell me, Hunny."

Hunny went for his cigarettes again, and this time he got one out of the pack. "I don't remember any of that O'Malley stuff at all. Oh Lord."

Shoemaker eased his chair back a foot or so as Hunny lit his Marlboro. "Hunny, you were just wonderful on O'Malley. You were the truth-teller. You were the free spirit. You were the unassimilated queer restoring the Whitmanesque joy of being free and gay and alive and at one with nature in a setting where gay people generally act defensive and bitter and defeated by the soulless and puritanical strictures of the medium."

Hunny shot smoke at Shoemaker and said, "Wow, if I was that good, I sure wish I could remember more of it."

"At the RDQ commune, you made us proud all over again to be sissies."

"I was a radical myself one time," Hunny said. "I didn't think of it that way at the time. I just thought of it as being pissed off and totally up to here with the New York Police Department. Artie was one, too. We were at Stonewall when the cops raided the place and we got arrested. Except for a few disorderly conduct things in the '80s, it's my only time to be arrested. It's where Artie and I met."

Shoemaker got down on the floor in front of Hunny. "Take your shoes off," he said. "I want to kiss your feet."

"Oh, that's all right."

Art said, "You should meet the twins. They'll probably drop by later."

Climbing back onto his chair, Shoemaker said, "Instead of your being shunned by gay America, Hunny, the Human Rights Campaign and all those other assimophiles should be hoisting you on their shoulders. It makes me want to weep, the way you're being treated by your own kind."

"Well, Quentin, it is disappointing. Especially with Mom missing and with so many other situations I'm currently dealing with. You won't believe what I'm putting up with. That's why Donald is here. I needed a detective just to deal with this incredible amount of crap. Donald, tell Quentin what we all have been going through since I won the lottery on Wednesday. It'll make your hair stand on end."

"All of it? Including the Cobleskill situation?"

"Yes, maybe Quentin has some ideas on how to deal with people who are just out-and-out satanic."

"Satanic! Let's hear about that. The Radical Drama Queens have ways of dealing with Lucifer's minions."

I described to Shoemaker the events of the past five days. I told him about the blackmail and other threats, the pellet-gun attack, Rita Van Horn's going missing, the kidnapping hoax, the laundry basket full of requests and demands for a share of Hunny's billion dollars, the smears from Bill O'Malley and the Family Preservation Association of Albany County, the lawsuits by FPAAC, Dave DeCarlo and Mason Doebler, and finally about the Brienings and Mrs. Van Horn's history with them and their loony extortion plot.

Shoemaker was especially interested in hearing about the Brienings. After I described them, he said, "Oh, yes, those two are agents of Satan, for sure." But he didn't seem worried about dealing with them, just amused and confident.

CHAPTER NINETEEN

Art had some mini-pizzas in the freezer that he microwaved for lunch. Nelson and Lawn dropped by briefly, but they didn't stick around and eat with us. Lawn plainly did not like the looks of Shoemaker, and it didn't help when Shoemaker asked Nelson if he was "one of the het Van Horns or one of the cocksucking Van Horns." Nelson replied that, yes, he and Lawn were "partners." Shoemaker waited until Nelson and Lawn had left the house before referring to them good-naturedly as "your average assimilationists."

"Their butt holes do make squeaking noises when they walk," Hunny said. "But Nelson is a good human, and there is even hope for Lawn if the SEC ever gets its act together."

"Is he a Wall Street crook?" Shoemaker asked.

"A total swindler."

"Another example of carrying cultural adaptation way too far."

Nelson had reported that Mrs. Van Horn was still missing from the nursing home, and Shoemaker said one of the RDQ people was a psychic and he would likely be willing to drive down and help find the old lady.

Hunny went pale again. "Isn't that just for finding bodies? We are pretty sure Mom is alive. At least that is our fervent hope."

"No, it wouldn't matter which world the lady is inhabiting. Ethan would probably be able to locate her spirit wherever it is."

"Would your psychic need one of her possessions or something?" Art asked. "That couch in the living room was Mother Van Horn's. Though we've had it for four or five years, and I suppose our scent is on it now. Antoine likes to stretch out on it. He's a friend of ours."

"No, it's not like a bloodhound," Shoemaker said. "But Ethan would need a photograph of the missing lady."

"There is one on top of the TV," Hunny said. "It's Mom in happier days. She's fluffy and sassy and she's got all her marbles. It was taken while Dad was still alive and the cancer hadn't been found."

Art said, "Hunny's father passed on at a relatively young age, sixty-four."

There was a knock at the front screen door, and a voice I recognized as Card Sanders' called, "Hello?"

Hunny whispered to Shoemaker, "It's the police. They don't know about the Brienings. Don't say anything. We don't want Mom to get arrested for embezzlement."

Shoemaker said, "Gotcha."

Art went out and led Sanders into the kitchen, and Hunny offered him some pizza. He said he'd had lunch, thanks, and he said he was sorry that there was still no word on Mrs. Van Horn's whereabouts. Sanders and Shoemaker were introduced, and Shoemaker said, "Sagittarius."

Sanders ignored this and said, "Right now, I'd like to speak with you, Mr. Van Horn, and Mr. Strachey privately, if there's someplace we can go."

"About Mom?" Hunny got shaky again and reached for a glass which wasn't there.

"Yes, about your mother."

"Anything you have to say about Mom you can say in front of Arthur, of course, and Mr. Shoemaker is my confidante."

"Are you his attorney?" Sanders asked Shoemaker.

"No, his good fairy."

Sanders said to Hunny, "I need to know about the Brienings."

Silence. Nobody moved.

"Just let's have it. What's the story with the Brienings?"

Hunny said, "Huh? The O'Briens?"

"No, Clyde and Arletta Briening. Mrs. Van Horn's former

employers at Crafts-a-Palooza in Cobleskill. I looked at your mother's work history, which is on file at Golden Gardens. For six years she was employed as a bookkeeper for the Brienings. Recently, Mr. Van Horn, you've been talking about giving the Brienings half your billion-dollar lottery payout. And on Bill O'Malley last night you told your mother that if she was watching, and if the Brienings had anything to do with her disappearance, she shouldn't worry, that you would deal with them. So, the question is, what's the story here? What am I not being told?"

Sanders leaned against the door frame and waited.

Hunny said, "This is very painful to talk about."

"Yes, but it could be helpful. All any of us in law enforcement want is to get your mom back in one piece. Just like you do, Mr. Van Horn."

"Believe me," Hunny said, "the Brienings have nothing to do with Mom being missing."

"That may well be. But in a missing persons case it is important for investigators to have a total profile of the subject. You never know when a piece of that profile that appears innocuous or irrelevant at first glance could turn out to be significant. Please just trust me on this, and if there's nothing useful here, so be it. I'm just intrigued as to why you're considering giving these Briening folks half a billion dollars. It's a fortune. They must be pretty important to you and your mother."

Hunny looked for his glass again and said, "They are."

We all watched Hunny.

"Do you promise that what I tell you will never be repeated? Not to anybody?"

"I can't really promise that, Mr. Van Horn. I'm not in a position to make such a guarantee. But I can say that confidentiality is an important part of any police investigation, both for ethical and practical reasons. I'll do everything within my power to guard whatever you tell me and make sure it will help, not hurt, you and your mother and this investigation."

Hunny looked down and mumbled something none of us could understand.

Sanders said, "Sorry?"

Hunny raised his head, squeezed his eyes shut, and said plainly, "Clyde Briening is my real father."

"Oh. Really?"

Art, standing by the sink, began studying the refrigerator magnets. One had a Tom of Finland drawing of a man with a penis the size of Quentin Shoemaker's left leg on it, and another had a picture of George W. Bush and the letters w-t-f.

Hunny said, "When my father was away at National Guard summer camp, my mother had one too many after dinner one night. She was a little too well lubricated for her own good. Lonely for some company, she committed adultery with Clyde, a neighbor at the time. Being a good Epworth League lady, Mom was not in the habit of doing this, and she never did it again, as far as any of us knows. I was born nine months later, and Dad was never good at math, so it never became an issue. Until, that is, I won the lottery. Then Clyde and Arletta got in touch and said they would spill the beans on Mom and on me unless I paid them half a billion dollars. Clyde says he has proof that I'm his son. He got a sample of my sperm — through a young visitor he sent here, but you don't want to hear about that — and he is having a DNA test done that will prove what he claims. He says it's only fair that his own flesh and blood spread the wealth around. He and Arletta are horrible people, but rather than risk embarrassing Mom, I may just pay them what they want. I'd still have half a billion left, a nice piece of change, and then Clyde and Arletta could just go...they could just go take a flying fuck at a donut!"

Sanders studied Hunny for a long moment. He said, "Jesus."

"Now you know. And now you know why I beg of you, Lieutenant, that none of this leaks out."

"Well, it does sound as if it is in the Brienings' interest that your mother returns safe and sound to the nursing home."

"Yes."

"But this is a form of extortion. Do you understand that?"

"I know, I know, and I don't *care*."

"Jesus."

"Sometimes families' dark secrets that have been buried should not be dug up. Like in *Suddenly Last Summer*. Liz Taylor went poking around in Montgomery Clift's past and was oh so sorry she ever took the trouble to be so curious."

Sanders said, "Well, it's your family, Mr. Van Horn. And your money."

"Right on both counts."

"But why did you say on Bill O'Malley that if the disappearance had anything to do with the Brienings, your Mom shouldn't worry, you would deal with them?"

Hunny looked at his lap again. *Mumble, mumble.*

"I beg your pardon?"

"Look, I was drunk on O'Malley. I didn't know what I was talking about. I don't have any kind of serious drinking problem, but I sometimes do toss a few back when I probably shouldn't, and then I say things that are confused or inappropriate. Arthur and I were just having a heart-to-heart about that subject this morning. I am actually off the sauce until Mom is back with me, and then we are going to cele-*brate*. And you are certainly invited to join us, Lieutenant."

Sanders looked over at me. I said, "Like Hunny says, now you know."

He kept looking at me. "Do I?"

"You know as much as I do."

Art said something about the day heating up again and asked us if anybody would like a root beer. We all accepted this nice offer, except for Detective Sanders, who left looking thoughtful.

CHAPTER TWENTY

Just after five in the afternoon, Nelson phoned with the news that the body of an elderly woman had been found in a wooded area in the town of Nassau. This was about six miles from East Greenbush. The dead woman was said to have been clad in a bathrobe and had no identification on her. She had not been dead long, and it was unclear whether the death had been from natural or other causes. The body was being kept temporarily in an ambulance near the site where it had been discovered, and Nelson said he was about to be driven over there to view the corpse and declare whether or not it was Rita Van Horn.

Hunny remained seated at the kitchen table, his head in his hands. Art sat next to him, an arm over Hunny's shoulders. No one had much to say. Occasionally, Hunny shook his head and cried quietly. "Oh, Mom, Mom."

Quentin Shoemaker had already driven back to Vermont to consult with the RDQ psychic and the commune's astrologer, but Marylou and the twins had arrived at the house. They stayed in the living room monitoring the local TV news. There had been a brief report about a woman's body being found in Nassau, but no details were yet available.

Hunny's sister Miriam phoned at one point, but she was hysterical and unable to speak for long.

Before the call from Nelson came, I had brought up the laundry basket from the basement and organized its contents on one end of the kitchen table. This was the heap of hundreds of letters, phone messages and e-mails that had arrived in the days following Hunny's lottery win begging for money or — in some cases — demanding cash in return for silence about some indiscretion or supposedly illegal act on Hunny's part. More letters had arrived that afternoon, a couple of them from national gay organizations pleading with Hunny not to make any more public appearances where he embarrassed the gay movement and "jeopardized the gains in public opinion and acceptance of gay men and women over recent decades," as one organization put it.

I made three piles, one called Deal With, another called Not Urgent, and a third — which included the letters from national gay organizations — called Go Fuck Yourself.

The Deal With pile contained a number of blackmail threats I had already defused. Or thought I had — Mason Doebler's lawsuit came as a rude surprise, and I could only surmise that he had been conned by a scuzzy lawyer into believing that he had a case. But now Hunny had his own scuzzy lawyer, a man I had recommended. A year earlier Bob Chicarelli had gotten me mixed up with a couple of Albany psychos whose case almost got Timmy thrown off a high balcony in Bangkok, Thailand. This guy owed me a favor.

While we waited to hear from Nelson, I sifted through the letters and notes looking for any possible connection, however remote, to Mrs. Van Horn's disappearance. None of the writers or callers mentioned her at all. A few of the extortion attempts urged Hunny to avoid embarrassing his family. But this seemed like generic blackmail-note language. There was no indication that any of these people even knew Hunny had parents to embarrass.

Two of the Deal With messages did seem worrisome. One was from an Albany man who claimed Hunny had given him gonorrhea in 1998, and he was sure he had named Hunny as a contact when he went to the STD clinic, and if he sued Hunny the clinic records would be subpoenaed. Plainly, this was just some jerk angling for an embarrassment-avoidance settlement — his threat was legally moronic — but I noted his name and contact information so that we could have a talk. Also in need of attention was the phone message left by an Albany man who claimed Hunny had promised him ten dollars if Hunny could photograph the man's genitalia with his cell phone. Hunny had not only reneged on the payment, the man said, but later a picture of the man's erect penis turned up on the Internet. Now he was thinking of suing Hunny but said he would consider an out-of-court settlement. I figured I would meet this one and give him ten dollars and a wedgie.

The Not Urgent pile consisted mainly of pleas for financial aid for good causes, less good causes and individuals whose requests would have to be considered case by case. Hunny's idea of setting up a foundation like Paul Newman and his wife Bea Arthur's was looking like the way to go.

The Go Fuck Yourself pile of messages included the ones from the gay organizations that were politely begging Hunny to cease to exist, as well as entirely silly requests like the one from the Albany man who asked for fifty dollars reimbursement for damage done to a valued article of the man's clothing. He said that in 1978 Hunny had spilled a glass of Jack Daniels on the man's cashmere sweater at the Playhouse, a long-defunct Central Avenue piano bar, and Hunny had never paid the man's dry-cleaning bill.

Sadly, the contents of the laundry basket were going to have to be dealt with in their various ways no matter how things went with Hunny's missing mom. There was also the unnerving possibility that Mrs. Van Horn had met with foul play, in which case Hunny would be legally obliged to hand the letters and messages over to the police for them to paw through. That could get ugly both for Hunny and for many of the schmoes, schlemiels and schmegeggies bent on grabbing hold of a piece of Hunny's unexpected bounty.

The phone rang four times while we waited to hear from Nelson. Two were press inquiries, and one was the Democratic Senate Campaign Fund calling again. Hunny was abrupt with all three callers and understandably harsh in his remarks to the Democrats.

The fourth call was from Stu Hood. Hunny was too upset to talk with Stu, who was told to call back on my cell phone so that Hunny's land line could be kept open.

Out on Hunny's back porch, I told Stu, "Look, you'll get your thousand dollars. But you have to be patient. Hunny's mother is still missing and that is the only thing he's thinking about at the moment. Haven't you heard about Mrs. Van Horn?"

"I don't think they get that channel at the Watering Hole. They just get wrestling."

"Well, it's a serious situation. A woman's body was discovered over in Nassau this afternoon, and it might be Mrs. Van Horn. We're waiting to hear from someone who went out to possibly identify the body. So you have to cool it, Stu. We'll be in touch later in the week about your thousand, and I'm guessing that you can figure out a way to scare up forty or fifty to tide you over in the meantime."

"Okay," Hood said, "but anyway I am seriously thinking of backing out of that agreement. A thousand dollars is not gonna do me much good, and I deserve a whole lot more. I heard Mason Doebler is going for the big money and he has a good chance of getting it. Somebody I know saw Mason on TV saying Hunny fucked him when he was an altar boy and Mason wants three million dollars or something. And Hunny wasn't even a priest, just some horny old troll in the park, so the fuckin' pope can't stop Mason from getting recompensed."

"Recompensed?"

"That's what I heard from the bartender here, James."

"Mason isn't getting a nickel, Stu. He's deluded. Is he drinking again, by chance?"

"I guess so. I saw him in here last night. He had a beer or three."

"Hunny never knew Mason when Mason was a boy. They met when Mason was over forty. This is all made up. It's a nuisance suit. That means he hopes Hunny will settle for less than the three hundred seventy-five million dollars Mason is claiming but more than the thousand Hunny offered him so Mason's car would pass inspection. Any lawyer who takes the case is doing so just to get on television so that when somebody needs a lawyer they might recognize that name in the yellow pages. It has nothing to do with law or justice. It's just advertising, and I hope you won't waste your time and money taking part in a cynical publicity stunt that'll never amount to anything else."

A little silence. I could hear voices and dance music in the background. "You are such a bullshitter, Strachey."

"Not in this case."

"I just feel like I've been treated like I'm a big nothing."

"No, Hunny wants to be fair. But you've been his trick, not his best friend since kindergarten. A sometime-trick can be a nice friendly thing in life. But it involves few ethical obligations — beyond the use of condoms when appropriate — and no legal obligations at all. The thousand dollars Hunny offered you — and still intends to pay you — is actually a very generous amount for someone in your position."

"No, it's not. You're forgetting that Hunny brought me out."

"Stu, you wouldn't really want to make that claim in court. It wouldn't work. Witnesses with other versions of your sexual history might come forward."

"Is that what you would call a threat?"

"I guess so, yes."

"Well, you better keep your fire hose handy."

"Don't say that, Stu. You don't know if this call is being recorded."

"Is it? Well, maybe I don't care. Maybe I'm going to get what I deserve for a change, a little respect. And maybe if I don't, there might be a big hot fire someplace, and somebody will get burnt up in it."

I knew I'd taken the wrong tack with Hood; threats just set him off. I was about to back off that approach and say some things I hoped he would find soothing when I heard a shriek from inside the house. I told Hood I had to go and would be in touch with him again soon and that I knew where to find him.

I rang off and went into the kitchen where Hunny was howling, not with grief but with joy and relief. Art said Nelson had just called, and the old lady's body found in Nassau was not Hunny's mom. It was a woman with Alzheimer's who had apparently wandered off from her vegetable-farm home nearby and suffered a fatal stroke or heart attack after she strolled into the woods.

Hunny decided the way to celebrate this news was with a "drinky-poo or possibly two," but Art pointed out that that didn't make sense since the dead lady's family might get wind of the celebration on Moth Street and be hurt and offended. Also, Art pointed out, Mrs. Van Horn was still missing.

"Oh, Arthur, girl, you had to go and remind me of that," Hunny moaned. "Oh, Mom, poor Mom, where can she *be*?"

Antoine, Marylou and the twins had all come into the kitchen, and Antoine suggested that they all join hands and pray.

Hunny said, "Antoine, honey, I'll try anything at this point."

We all joined hands and bowed our heads, and Hunny said, "Lord, help get Mom's wrinkly old butt back to Golden Gardens ASAP, 'cause this whole dumb lottery thing plus Mom taking off somewhere has just about wrecked my last nerve, and I don't think I can take much more of this horse doody. In Jesus' name, amen. Oh, one more thing. Smite the Brienings, okay?"

Then everybody said amen.

CHAPTER TWENTY-ONE

"I heard at the office," Timmy said, "that all kinds of gay organizations are trying to get Hunny to lower his profile, or at least to quit acting like such an obnoxious drunken screaming queen in public. People are upset over — to cite one bloodcurdling example — the anti-gay-marriage forces in Maine running TV ads with pictures of Hunny and his Marylou Whitney impersonator and asking Maine voters if these are the people they want teaching their schoolchildren."

"Neither Hunny nor Marylou is a teacher. Hunny is newly retired from BJ's Warehouse, and Marylou is an independently wealthy Palm Beach and Saratoga socialite. So Maine's schoolchildren are safe."

"The gay-marriage referendum up there is expected to be close, and it really doesn't help the image of gay people to have Hunny falling-down drunk on television and yelling into the cameras about some drag queen's penis."

"Yes, Hunny behaved very badly on his Focks News debut. I was embarrassed and ashamed right along with the rest of gay America. But Hunny was goaded into that response by O'Malley, who's the real problem here. O'Malley and all the homophobic half-wits who watch him and believe whatever nutty stuff comes out of his mouth. Although, Hunny's perfectly understandable response to O'Malley was strategically unwise, I will concede."

"It's more than just strategy. It's decency. It's sobriety. It's sanity. It's taste."

We were in the kitchen fixing a quick dinner before I went back up to Moth Street. Timmy had brought home a barbecued chicken from a place on Lark Street, and I had shucked some fresh corn and was making water boil in a pot, my speciality in the kitchen.

I said, "Taste is overrated."

"Yes, but sanity isn't. Or sobriety."

I told Timmy about Quentin Shoemaker and the RDQ and their standing up against assimilationism.

"Assimilationism? Some people would call living the way we do, and the way most of our friends do, having a life. A good life, actually. A life where we can get up in the morning and not have to think about getting called names or arrested or where our next orgasm is coming from. We can just think about the good and bad minutiae of being human, as well as the bigger questions of human affairs, and not be saddled with some desperate quest for endless stimulation or having to make everybody you meet feel like they want to run out of the room."

"That's a pretty bleak assessment of the way a lot of gay people have lived for a pretty long time. Basically, people like Hunny are just like us and the people we know. They get up every day and go to work, and at the end of the day and on weekends they want a little comfort and diversion. They just do it with more humor and a cruder style than most gay people do. And most straight people."

"Much of the trouble has to do mainly with style, yes. I grant you that. It's not my style, though, and it's not yours. And it's a style that causes trouble a-plenty for the rest of us when it turns up in anti-gay TV ads in Maine."

I said, "Should corn be boiled for three minutes or five?"

"Three is plenty. Aunt Moira always said twenty minutes, but her corn was so tough only her hog could eat it."

"She kept a hog?"

"My cousin Kevin."

"Shoemaker talks about Hunny and Art as being natural and free and in touch with their inner child. There's a lot of truth to this, and I enjoy them and even sort of envy them whenever I'm not cringing."

"I sometimes find that humor and playfulness refreshing, too, but it's the relentlessness that gets to me after a while. And the always sexualizing everything. Give it a break, I always want to say."

"Maybe they are just more honest than the rest of us."

"Oh, Donald, please. At this late date, are you going to go hippie on me?"

"I mean honest in the sense that they are in touch not so much with their inner child as their inner Sigmund Freud. Sexuality is always going on, and people like Hunny and Art are just more aware and comfortable with the phenomenon than most of us. And they've learned not to be afraid of it but to have fun with it. They're more like the Thais in that respect, except in Thailand people are not so crude about it or so insistent."

"Exactly. They have a sense of proportion. They may be in touch with their inner child, but they are also comfortable with their outer grown-up."

"Well, Hunny and Art's way of life is a part of gay culture that I hope never disappears. The self-destructive parts of it I could do without — all the alcohol especially — but the gather-ye-rosebuds-while-ye-may spirit makes a lot of sense for getting people through this…I don't want to say vale of tears. For most of the lucky ones like you and me, it's not that at all."

"'Cockeyed caravan of life,'" Timmy said. "I think that's what you mean, especially in Hunny's case. Preston Sturges in the script for *Sullivan's Travels* talks about our passage on this plane of existence as 'the cockeyed caravan of life.' The cockeyed caravan does seem to be thriving in one of its most esoteric and at the same time least inhibited forms over on Moth Street."

"I just hope," I said, "that Hunny can survive his more-hectic-than-most expressions of unassimilated queerdom. It's a life that though it has its rewards for some people, it also takes a toll."

"A price must be paid."

"I've made some mild stabs at getting Hunny to moderate his behavior, but he has a way of making me feel like Aunt Polly to his Tom Sawyer."

Timmy said, "That corn must be done."

"Right."

"Donald, I have a lot of trouble thinking of Hunny as a character out of Twain. Boyd MacDonald maybe. Or William S. Burroughs."

"Oh no, not Burroughs. Hunny is alert, alive, and I think I can even say truly happy."

My cell phone went off, and when I saw that it was Hunny calling I was tempted not to answer it. But I guessed that it was some new awful mess that Hunny had created or stepped in or had land on him, and I was right.

CHAPTER TWENTY-TWO

The Brienings were at it again. They had phoned Nelson and told him that they had read on somebody's Internet blog that Rita Van Horn's disappearance was a hoax, just as Bill O'Malley suspected it was. Mrs. Van Horn, the blogger reported, had been spotted in a motel in the town of Lake George where she was staying under an assumed name. Obviously, Arletta Briening told Nelson, this was all part of a scheme to delay or even avoid paying the Brienings the half billion dollars they were owed. When Nelson insisted that the Van Horns knew nothing of this, Arletta said she was sure the report was reliable because the information came from one of her FPAAC friends and they were honest people.

"Did the blogger give the name of the motel?" I asked Nelson.

I was back at the house on Moth Street, where Nelson and Lawn had arrived in person to deliver news of the new threat from the Brienings.

"No, he didn't. I asked Arletta and she said no."

"This is probably somebody's malicious imagination at work. Do you have the blog URL?"

Hunny said, "What's a URL? Is that like 'you are luscious' in e-mail language?"

"No, Uncle Hunny, it isn't."

Nelson had the address at blogspot, and while Lawn sat by the kitchen phone scanning the *Financial Times*, Art, Hunny, Nelson and I went upstairs to Hunny and Art's room, where they kept their computer on what might have been somebody's boyhood desk. Hunny and Art had a double bed with a veneer headboard that looked like Richard Widmark might have slept in it in *Kiss of Death*. Clothing was heaped around the room and tumbling out of closets. A bookcase contained only a few books — some paperback movie guides and a glossy photo book called *Butt Boys of Budapest*. The flat-screen TV was nearly identical to the one in the living room downstairs.

Art went online and found the blog called Blood of Tyrants, a right-wing anti-Obama bilge-fest. It was the work of someone calling himself Tom In Paine. In addition to the flag-draped anti-tax and pro-gun screeds, there were stories on "typical" gays as child molesters and links to ex-gay ministries.

A posting from that morning described Bill O'Malley's "expose" of "Huntington Van Horn's gay lifestyle" and the FPAAC suit against the lottery for spreading "perversion and immorality." Tom In Paine credited O'Malley for first revealing that a missing persons report involving Hunny's mother was actually a publicity stunt concocted to obtain a TV reality show contract, like the recent balloon-boy hoax. The blogger stated that Mrs. Van Horn was in hiding at a Lake George motel. She had been spotted coming and going by an FPAAC member who had seen her photo on the O'Malley show when Hunny was waving it around. The motel was not named.

I said, "There must be dozens of motels in Lake George. Tom In Paine had to know that this would be hard for us or anybody else to check out and refute."

"Mom enjoys Lake George,' Hunny said, "but I think this is just a pack of lies."

"I'm sure you're right, Uncle Hunny. Most of the stuff on these right-wing blogs is pure fiction. But I know Mother and Grandma used to go up to Lake George and ride around on a paddleboat and stay at a place near the lake where they liked the stuffed haddock at the restaurant across the street. It might be a good idea if somebody rode up there and just took a look."

I asked Nelson if he knew the name of the motel.

"No, but Mother would know."

"Antoine doesn't go in to work till four o'clock tomorrow, so maybe he and the twins could ride up there. Tyler and Schuyler could work on their homework in the car."

'Well, we really have to do everything possible to get Grandma Rita back quickly," Nelson said. "Arletta reiterated to me that their deadline is Wednesday for the half billion to be turned over. In fact, she said noon Wednesday, not a minute later."

Hunny flicked an ash from his lit cigarette into the ashtray on top of the computer, whose keyboard was brown with nicotine stains. "Oh Lord, all we need is for the Brienings to distribute letters out at Golden Gardens calling Mom a crook right before she walks in the door out there or she is found in a hospital in New Jersey waking up from a coma."

"Why New Jersey?" I asked.

"Because that's where Karen Ann Quinlan was in her coma."

"New Jersey, the coma state," Art said. "It's on the license plates."

"I am thinking more and more," Hunny said, "that maybe I should just give the Brienings the half a billion dollars. That money isn't even real to me anyways. I would never miss it. And then we could just concentrate on getting Mom back and not have the Brienings hanging over our heads and breathing down our necks."

"That is what Mother prefers," Nelson said. "But that's easy for her to say, because she and Dad have nice pensions from the county. No, I think you've been right, Uncle Hunny, to try to keep the money away from those terrible people. Lawn has some ideas on how you can invest it that he wants to discuss with you, but of course that can easily wait until we have resolved the situation with Grandma Rita."

"I am just so grateful," Hunny said, "that that poor old lady over in Nassau wasn't Mom. I never imagined Mom dying like that. Out in the woods, I mean. She doesn't like nature as much as she likes comfy and cozy and a good time. She's always preferred town over country."

Art said, "That lady who died was a farmer. Maybe she went the way she always wanted to go."

"I can see Mom keeling over at Applebee's with a huge plate of nachos in front of her. She would be dying happy."

"Like mother, like son," Art said. "A fatal helping of Applebee's nachos sounds like just the ticket for you, dear one. In fact, include me in. Or would we rather die in the sack with a pair of humpy rugby players sitting on our faces?"

Hunny laughed. "That's a tough one."

Nelson shot a glance at me — he badly wanted me to be his ally in disapproving of Hunny and Art's far-from-Noel-Coward-like sexual humor — but I found myself letting him down, and I was almost sorry I could not oblige. Though I did hope that Hunny could find a way to contain himself in the future when on national television.

"Well, let's get going then," Nelson said. "Lawn and I are driving back over to East Greenbush to see how Mother is doing, and I guess you'll be talking to Antoine. Right, Uncle Hunny? I'll get the name of the motel."

"Yes, but I do have to do one thing. My old boss at BJ's called earlier and said most of the staff had quit because I was going to give them all a million dollars. The managers are having trouble both with stocking and at the checkouts, and Earl asked me if I would urge the gals and guys to come back temporarily and then give a week's notice after I presented them with their checks. I said I would do that for the sake of the customers who are apparently waiting an eternity to get out to the parking lot with their three hundred rolls of toilet paper, so I have to make a few phone calls."

"Okay."

"One other thing, Nelson. Tell Lawn I will invest some money with him — maybe a million or so — as a favor to you and my sister. But the bulk of my fortune, whether or not it includes the half a billion the Brienings are after, is going to be placed in safe investments that are socially responsible. I was just thinking about this after something Arthur said, and my plan is to invest heavily in — for one thing — Applebee's. TGI Friday's also, even though it has some unpleasant associations for me now, what with the kidnapping scam and the TGI's Dumpster's role in that. But I love their nachos, too. I just want you and Lawn to understand that this is the first time anybody in our family ever had such a huge amount of money, and I simply am not about to take any chances with it."

Nelson did not sigh or roll his eyes over this announcement. He looked as if he could not figure out for the life of him exactly how to respond.

CHAPTER TWENTY-THREE

Quentin Shoemaker and eight of his Radical Drama Queen friends arrived around eleven that night. They had a big wooden box full of the paraphernalia Quentin said they would need for any "action" that might be called for. Among the six was Ethan Kulak, the RDQ's psychic, and Savion Davenport, the commune's astrologer. Kulak was even tinier than Shoemaker, with intense black eyes and a small round mouth that made him look as if he was always about to say something starting with a *W*. Davenport was also skinny, and had a brown bony face and enough dreadlocks for a small sheep to get lost in. The communards were all in raggedy shorts or jeans and T-shirts, except for a rugged older man named Graham who wore a Hawaiian grass skirt and halter top.

Antoine had gone off to work the overnight shift at Golden Gardens, but Marylou and the twins were in the living room monitoring the eleven o'clock local newscasts for any reports on Mrs. Van Horn, or any new outbreaks of anti-Hunny activity. The rest of us gathered in the kitchen, where Shoemaker astonished Hunny, Art and me by declaring, "Ethan and Savion have consulted the heavens, the spiritual and energy flows, and each other. And they can say with some degree of certainty, Hunny, that your mother is at the present moment in the town of Lake George."

"Whoa. Really?"

"That's amazing," Art said.

Kulak had placed the photograph of Mrs. Van Horn that Shoemaker borrowed earlier in the center of the kitchen table. She grinned up at us, and just at the bottom of the frame was the top of a cocktail glass with a swizzle stick peeking out.

"Whereabouts in Lake George?" Hunny asked. "And what is she doing? Is she well? Is she being held captive or anything?"

"Your mother is asleep right now," Kulak said. "So it wouldn't be good to call her even if we had her number. She is healthy and contented but somewhat worn out."

"Wow. How can you tell that?"

"Savion Googled her name, and that helped. There was some kind of blog saying she had been seen in Lake George."

Hunny's face drooped. "Oh. You're getting your information from Tom In Paine. Now I don't know. That guy is an idiot."

"Yes, I know he is, but we confirmed the sighting," Davenport said. "Your mother's sign of Jupiter is entering the seventh house, and today is August seventeenth, so she is sure to be equidistant between Saratoga Springs and Schroon Lake. That has to be Lake George."

Hunny looked at Art, who shrugged. "Why the hell not?"

I said, "So you guys have a wireless laptop you carry around to make your calculations?"

"I've got my Blackberry," Shoemaker said. "And Ethan has his human mind."

I said, "So, Ethan, can your human mind come up with an address for us where Mrs. Van Horn can be found?"

Nelson had phoned earlier to tell us that the motel where Rita and Miriam Van Horn used to like to stay was called the Silvery Moon. We had let Antoine know about that, but no one else had yet been told.

Kulak said, "I am fairly sure it's the Super 8, but I'm not one hundred percent certain."

"Hunny and Art's friend Antoine, along with Tyler and Schuyler, who you met out in the other room, are going to take a drive up to Lake George in the morning to try to check out the supposed sighting of Mrs. Van Horn. Maybe a couple of you could ride along and add your extrasensory GPS."

The RDQers agreed to do that and asked if they could spend the night in Art and Hunny's house. They said they had their Tibetan prayer mats they could sleep on, and they had brought their own dried head cheese breakfast cakes. Hunny said, sure, there was plenty of room. I said they were also welcome to Hunny and Art's guest room and I would spend the night at home. I thought about inviting some of them to come over and spread their mats out at the foot of Timmy's and my bed but concluded that Timmy's bemusement might be limited.

I asked Hunny to walk with me out to my car. It was a hot moonlit buggy August night on Moth Street. We passed the two security guys sitting on the porch, and one of them said to me, "Are those hippies?"

"You could call them that. I doubt if they would use the word."

"They look like they are."

"That word is mostly used now for revivals of *Hair*. These guys aren't actors. They're genuine."

"I just wondered."

When we got out to my car, I said to Hunny, "You know, Quentin and his crew are full of shit."

"I thought they might be."

"They are good and sweet and decent, but they have no more idea where your mother is than Bill O'Malley does, or the balloon boy."

"I know. But Quentin is nice to me and he doesn't treat me like I'm a bad gay person and a traitor to gays just because I'm so fun-loving and enjoy a stiff one once in a while. Oh, I mean drink," he added and chortled.

"I wasn't sure."

"Are you sure you wouldn't like a nice blowjob, Donald?"

"No."

"It relieves tension."

"I'm aware of that."

"I guess you're getting it at home."

"That's part of it."

"Variety is nice."

"I can't deny that."

"Well, maybe some of the RDQ boys will be up for a romp."

"Hard to say."

"Donald, girl, do you think I should tell them to go back to Vermont? They aren't going to be much help, it looks like. But I like having Quentin around to boost my morale. I love that he wanted to lick my feet. At first, I thought, oh, what a weirdo. But he wasn't referring to shrimping, I don't think. He meant to show his respect."

"He admires you a lot. And he's not alone."

"Oh, I know. Not everybody's dumping on me. All the gals out at BJ's have called and expressed their heartfelt wishes about Mom, and some said I should have kicked Bill O'Malley in the balls. A lot of the gang we normally see at Rocks on Saturday night have been supportive, calling and sending nice cards. I heard that some radio program in Troy called *Homo Radio* said nice things about me. It's just phonies like Nelson and Lawn and that type of straight-acting gay person who have been pissing all over Artie and me."

"I don't know that they're all phonies. They just find your uninhibitedness and your...zest for life a little scary."

"Well, tough titty. Anyway, they are so phonies. I would never tell Nelson — he is so innocent and it would break his heart — but Artie saw Lawn one time out behind a Thruway rest stop getting his dick sucked by a state assemblyman from Buffalo who had just had his picture in the paper for getting a prize from the Boy Scouts."

"That sounds complicated. But a lot of guys really are monogamous and very comfortable with the old-fashioned two-people-devoted-to-each-other model. It's safe and comfortable and emotionally rewarding. Biology being biology, some of them may slip once in a while. But overall they aren't particularly hypocritical. They live the way they live not just for convention's sake but for love."

"Oh, Donald, darlin', you obviously haven't seen what I've seen. For a detective, you don't seem to have been around the block all that much. And anyway, don't tell me about love. If there's any love in this world truer than Artie's and mine, I would be very surprised to see it. We have two brains and two dicks but only one funny soul. Our two hearts beat as one. When one of us croaks, the other one will drop dead in about two seconds. We share everything from money to boys to sorrows to nacho supremes at Applebee's. We know so much about love that there ain't nothin' that you or Nelson or even Branjolina can teach us on that subject, not one single thing. So when I get criticized for the way I talk or drink or carry on, I don't like it — it hurts my feelings, it really does — but I know I have love in my life and because of that I know I can stand just about anything."

I drove home and told Timmy, who was half asleep, about the RDQ guys arriving and about what Hunny had told me about him and Art and their — marriage was the best word for it. Timmy heard what I was saying about Hunny and Art and squeezed my hand. He also said he was truly grateful that I had not brought any Tibetans home to sleep on the floor at the foot of our bed.

CHAPTER TWENTY-FOUR

I was barely awake myself when the phone rang at seven thirty in the morning. It was Card Sanders and his tone was cool.

"I just checked with East Greenbush. There's no sign yet of Mrs. Van Horn."

"Jeez. This is really getting worrisome. Has the FBI been brought in yet?"

"No, because there's no indication of foul play. Huntington's mother is just an old lady who wandered out the front door of a nursing home. In fact, there's no indication of anything at all. She just went poof. It's very odd."

"That's what it looks like. But with no corpse having turned up, it sure looks as if somebody picked her up. But who? Family and friends all deny any contact with her, and surely strangers giving her a ride would have seen news reports and alerted the sheriff."

I was in the kitchen with my juice and muffin, the *Times Union* spread out on the counter, and Timmy was upstairs performing his before-work extensive toilette.

Sanders said, "I'm still curious about these people the Brienings who Mrs. Van Horn used to work for."

"How come?"

"For one thing, Mr. Van Horn told me he is considering giving the Brienings half a billion dollars because Clyde Briening is his biological father."

"It's a strange, heartbreaking story."

"Yeah, but more strange than heartbreaking."

"How so?"

"For one thing, when Hunny Van Horn was born, Clyde Briening was just eight years of age."

"Nah, that couldn't be."

"That's right, Strachey. Fathering a child at that age is pretty close to being biologically impossible. But I checked the ages of both men."

"It would make it into Ripley's."

"I am relieved that Mrs. Van Horn didn't have an affair with an eight-year-old."

"You bet."

"So then what's the real deal with the Brienings? I'm nagged by Mr. Van Horn's saying on Bill O'Malley — I've TiVoed it five times now — that if his mother's disappearance had anything to do with the Brienings, not to worry, that he would deal with them. I'm thinking strongly now that there is a connection, and I'm also thinking strongly that you know exactly what that connection is. No? If I'm mistaken, please explain to me how I've failed to grasp the obvious."

"Look," I said, meaning it, "if there was a connection, why wouldn't I tell you and all the other law enforcement folks so that you all could wrap up this whole missing person sad situation pronto? It is possible that the Brienings might have spooked Mrs. Van Horn in some way and she took off for wherever she took off to. But I have spoken with the Brienings. And believe me, they don't have Mrs. Van Horn in their custody, and they don't know where she is. It's to their advantage that she be safe and in the tender arms of the staff at Golden Gardens so that Clyde and Arletta can go ahead and press Hunny for the half billion. Having her running around loose and exposed to possible danger is exactly what they do not desire. Don't you see what I'm saying, Lieutenant?"

"I do see, and it would be really insensitive of me to go out to Cobleskill and question the Brienings if Clyde really was Mr. Van Horn's father and I stirred up some ugly family mess that's none of my business or the business of the police in any way. But Mr. Van Horn was obviously lying when he told me that real-father bullshit story. So why don't you allay my growing suspicions by telling me the fucking truth about this family of psychopathic liars for a change?"

I said, "Okay, look. I do know a little more. That must be obvious. But if you knew the truth it would just place you in an ethical bind that you really don't want to be in. You know people in the department who know me, and they can vouch for me. They can tell you that if I say you're better off not knowing everything there is to know about the Brienings and the Van Horns, then you can trust that assessment. Just ask."

Sanders snorted. "Strachey, I'm a police officer, not a third-grader who needs to be kept out of an R-rated movie. Just fucking tell me what's going on here."

I said, "I can't."

"Why?"

"I've explained that. You might be obligated to report something to the DA. In the end, it would all turn out okay for the Van Horns and not so great for the Brienings, I feel confident. But this has to do with family image and standing with church ladies and small-town embarrassment and shame. The legal part of it is the least of it. Or is according to the Van Horns. And it's their decision to make."

I could hear Sanders breathing. He said, "Hunny Van Horn is concerned about image? This I find hard to believe."

"With your indulgence, I can't really say any more."

"One of the Van Horns did something to the Brienings that was so bad that it's worth half a billion dollars to the Van Horns to cover up. For that amount of money, it must have been murder."

"You'd think so."

"Of course, these days celebrities like Mr. Van Horn can get away with pretty much anything. You get drunk and shove a school bus off a cliff, and then you go on Barbara Walters and cry and get a nice book deal and maybe serve a month in the county lockup and then you get out and bake sheet cakes at a soup kitchen, and that's all there is to it. What's this embarrassment and shame stuff? They don't exist anymore. Haven't the Van Horns heard about that?"

"They are not culturally up-to-date, Lieutenant."

"Mrs. Van Horn, once she's back, she could get a stand-up comedy gig on Jay Leno. At Golden Gardens, the staff all say she's the joke lady. I was over there, and I had a hard time getting people to talk about Rita because all they wanted to do was tell me how funny she is and how she keeps everybody on the staff in stitches."

The "joke lady"? This all sounded familiar, and I made a mental note to ask Antoine and Hunny about a phone call Mrs. Van Horn had received — in fact a series of phone calls — that suddenly seemed important.

CHAPTER TWENTY-FIVE

When I got over to Hunny's house, Marylou had gone off to work at the tax department and Antoine had already picked up the twins and two of the RDQ guys — the ones with the mental GPS capabilities — and headed up to Lake George. Shoemaker and the other communards went out for a walk through the North End, Hunny said. The night before they had seen a Hummer parked in someone's driveway, and they wanted to see if they could levitate it and shake the evil spirits out.

Hunny told me he had talked to the sheriff's department in East Greenbush and there was still no clue as to what had become of his mother. He said the officers were feeling frustrated and more and more worried, and so was he.

I asked, "Did Lieutenant Sanders call you?"

"No."

"He called me. He found out that Clyde Briening was eight years old when you were born."

"Whoopsy daisy."

"Yeah."

"That Clyde. What a stud. Ooo-eee. So the detective knows I fibbed? Oh boy."

"I told him you were only protecting the family from unnecessary embarrassment over a matter he need not concern himself with. But he will continue to pick at this scab, so be ready."

"Oh, Donald, girl, I'm just so scared Mom is going to be found — her mind gone, and working next to the ovens at Arby's or something — and the cops are going to rush in with their Tasers drawn and arrest her for embezzlement in front of all her new friends. Or she shows up at Golden Gardens just when the Brienings waltz in and write on the name card outside her door *Mrs. Thief Van Horn* and all the old gals out there will start treating her like some seedy shoplifter and calling her Ma Barker. You know, it would be so easy to just drive out to Cobleskill and write a check for half a billion dollars and throw it in Clyde and Arletta's face. And that would be that. Tomorrow is their deadline, so-called, and that is what I am so, so tempted to just go ahead and do."

Art came downstairs and into the kitchen. Hunny said, "Have a nice poop, dear one?"

Art shrugged. "Eh. So-so."

"Artie, I am thinking of paying off the Brienings. I am just sick of that whole situation. Would you mind if we only ended up with five hundred million dollars? We'd still be on easy street, heaven knows. That cute cop, Sanders, is closing in on Mom and her misdeed. She's like Jimmy Cagney in *White Heat.* I hate to reward evil people, but one day the Brienings will meet their maker and they'll get theirs real good. I'd love to be there to watch it, but of course I don't know which place I am going to end up in."

"I wouldn't pay them a red cent, Hunny. It's not the money, it's the principle. Anyway, I just thought of something. For a lot less than half a billion dollars you could probably bribe the Albany County DA. It's not like the old days when you could buy a judge or DA around here for fifty thou. But I'll bet a hundred million would get you all the deal you'd need. And the Brienings could just take a hike. And for goodness sakes, you can afford it."

Hunny brightened. "Oh, Artie, girl, you just might be right. I should run that by Nelson and Lawn. They know all those people. They are crooks just like the people they eat with at Jack's. They're all conniving peas in a pod."

"This is a bad idea," I said. "It's illegal, it's immoral and it's dangerous. In Albany, it's not 1950 anymore. Hunny, you could end up with federal charges and then your mother would really be embarrassed."

"Oh. No, I don't want to end up in Danbury as somebody's white bitch."

"Nuh-uh," Art said. "Connecticut has gay marriage now, but in the federal pen you wouldn't necessarily get to choose."

"Then I just think I have to pay them," Hunny said.

"Maybe you're right, luv. And your tough-guy private eye here still refuses to have the Brienings offed. Is that still your position, Donald?"

"Yes, homicide is out. The impulse is understandable, but the deed would have consequences."

"Anyway," Art said, "Quentin Shoemaker said this morning that he and his hippies have a plan for the Brienings."

"They do?"

"I heard them talking about it out in the hall when I was in the bathroom for my first BM."

"What plan?" I asked.

"Some kind of exorcism."

"That should help."

"Donald," Hunny said, "you don't have any faith in the RDQ boys, I can tell. But their hearts are in the right place, you have to admit."

"I admit that. And I like them. I even admire them in a lot of ways. But they're not going to help with the Brienings, and they're not going to get your mother back. People with a firmer grip on reality are going to do both of those things, if anybody is."

"You don't seem to have any better ideas," Art said. "How much was your fee?"

I ignored that — reasonable as the question was — and asked Hunny if he had a list of all the friends and family members who had been queried about Mrs. Van Horn's disappearance.

"Sure. I stuck it in the back of the phone book. Do you want to see it?"

"Please."

Hunny was at the kitchen table sucking down his fifth

Marlboro of the day according to the evidence in the ashtray. He extracted a Domino's Pizza take-out menu that had been stuffed in his Albany County phone book and flipped it over. Written in pen on the back was a long list of names. I scanned the list.

I said, "Who is your mother's friend who calls her once a week with a fresh supply of jokes?"

"That would be Tex Clermont. But she is not on the list."

"Why not? She sounds like a close friend."

"She is, but Tex — Eileen is her actual name — lives in assisted living in Houston. She's not around here."

"Who is she? What's their relationship?"

"When Tex was married to her fourth husband, Roberto, they lived in Albany. He was a state trooper. But when Cuatro croaked — that's what Tex called him, Numero Cuatro — Tex moved back to Texas to be near her daughter down there."

"So Tex and your mom were pals?"

"Oh, they did everything together. They met at the racetrack, so they did a lot of playing the ponies, and they went down to Foxwoods sometimes to hit the tables. Mom really missed Tex when she moved back to Houston."

"Does Tex ever visit up here?"

"Not that I ever heard of," Hunny said. "What are you thinking? That maybe Tex is the person who picked Mom up and took her somewhere? I would doubt that. Tex has bad hips and uses a walker. I know she doesn't drive. Mom has told me how grateful she is that even if she is losing her mind, at least she isn't in the kind of pain Tex is in. Mom doesn't move so great either, but at least she is not in agony whenever she tries to move."

Art said, "Being old is a load of crap."

"Maybe," I said, "even if Mrs. Clermont hasn't taken your mom somewhere, maybe she has been in touch with her or has some idea where your mother might have gone. It sounds as though they're real chums."

"We could check."

"Do you have a number or address?"

"No, that information would be in Mom's address book in her room."

"Could you call Mrs. Kerisiotis and ask her to have someone check?"

Hunny said he would do that, and he made the call. Mrs. Kerisiotis's secretary said the administrator wasn't in her office but they would call Hunny back with the information he wanted.

"Everyone at Golden Gardens is really upset about Mom," Hunny said. "People think she might have been snatched, or drug gangs got her, or even vampires, Antoine told me. They watch all those vampire shows on TV. I don't think old people should be allowed to watch that stuff. It's too upsetting."

"If it was too upsetting, they wouldn't look at it," Art said. "They must like the immortality part of it."

"And the physical contact. People of all ages appreciate a little physical affection."

The phone rang and Hunny snatched it up. "Van Horn residence. Oh, Antoine, honey-doll! Any luck? Any trace of Mom? Uh-huh. Uh-huh. Oh, girl! Oh, you can't be serious! Oh, God, hold on a sec. I have to tell Artie!"

Hunny said to Art and me, "Antoine says they checked the Silvery Moon Motel and didn't see Mom. And the clerk wouldn't say who was staying there, saying it's against the law to give out that information. But there's a beach down behind the motel, and you'll never guess who's the lifeguard there!"

Art asked who.

"Sean Shea. He used to go out with Ellis Feebeaux, who works out at BJ's. Sean is famous for the tattoo on his dick that's a picture of Cardinal Egan."

"It's not a perfect likeness," Art said. "But if you think about it, you can see that's who it is."

Hunny asked Antoine, "So did you show the RDQ boys Sean's tat? I know the twins have seen it. Uh-huh. Uh-huh. Well, look around and maybe Ethan there, the one with the crystal ball, has some ideas. Right. Right. Okay, tood-lee-oo."

"No sign of Mother Van Horn?" Art asked.

"No, but they are going over to the Super Eight where Ethan thinks Mom is staying. The thing is, the desk clerks can't give out guest information."

"I'll bet they would for twenty-five thousand dollars."

"Oh, that's an idea. If I'm so rich, I suppose I should start acting like it."

"Did the Vermont boys enjoy Sean's tattoo?"

"They went into the men's room, Antoine said, and had a quick look-see. But it was hard to make out. Sean had just been in the water, and that lake is cold."

Art said, "Sean is an excellent lifeguard, but he is not a very good Catholic."

The phone rang again and Hunny answered it. He had a brief exchange, wrote something down on his Domino's menu and hung up.

"That's Mrs. Kerisiotis's girl calling back. They got Mom's address book and found Tex Clermont's number."

I suggested to Hunny that he give his mom's buddy a call and ask her if she had heard from Mrs. Van Horn or if she even knew that she was missing.

Hunny said, "This is outside our calling area, but I guess I can afford to call anywhere I please."

He dialed and soon had an exchange with someone who apparently was not Tex Clermont. Hunny exclaimed a number of times and told the person who answered Mrs. Clermont's phone about his mother's disappearance and why he was calling. Then he said he thought the police in both Texas and New York ought to be notified and hung up.

"Eileen Clermont has also disappeared," Hunny said to Art and me. "This is just incredible. She's been gone since last Thursday, and the police are looking for her, and everybody down there is just worried sick."

"I thought she was on a walker," Art said, "and couldn't get around."

"I talked to the nurse that answered Tex's phone, and she said that one of the home's aides is missing too. They think he might have taken Tex somewhere because they were always pals and joked about running off and getting married. The aide's name is Herero Flores, and his family and friends are worried about him, too."

"It would be useful to know, " I said, "if Herero Flores has a car and if so what kind."

I asked Hunny for the nursing home number he had used and then made a series of calls on my cell.

Ten minutes later I said to Hunny, "I think we're going to get your mom back."

"I have a feeling you're right, Donald. I think all our thoughts and prayers are soon to be answered. But just in time, I'm afraid, for the Brienings to work their evil on Mom and on all the rest of the Van Horns. I have only twenty-four hours before the Brienings go after Mom, and I'm afraid I have no choice but to fork over half a billion dollars, tomorrow morning at the latest."

I told Hunny I had one more idea on how to deal with the Brienings, and it didn't involve exorcism.

CHAPTER TWENTY-SIX

By six that evening I was set up in Cobleskill and ready to take possession of the original document in which Rita Van Horn had confessed to embezzling sixty-one thousand dollars from the Brienings. It was like the situation in *The Letter*, the Maugham story and Bette Davis movie, except I was not going to pay a lot of money for the letter and then get knifed in the gut anyway. I was going to create a distraction that would lure the Brienings out the front door of their store, and I was going to go in the back door and take away the lock box where they told me the letter had been secured.

The crew I had assembled met me at the McDonald's on the eastern edge of town. Marylou was there but not in drag. She was in a business suit and looked like the average middle-aged accountant you might expect to find at the New York State Department of Taxation.

Accompanying her were several people I recognized from the two lottery-prize celebrations at Hunny's house, the one broadcast on Channel 13 six days earlier and then the Saturday night bacchanal the neighbors had complained about. All of these people were in go-to-work professional or blue-collar gear. The only thing that might have distinguished them from typical commuters on the way home after a summer work day was this: close up some of the men looked as if they might have been women, and some of the women looked as if they might have been men.

Marylou had on a name tag that read *Buzz Beasley, Simon & Schuster*. Others had name tags, too, that were whimsical — Tom Cruise, Britney Spears, Senator Charles Grassley — and they were all gathered around a van with a big sign on the side that read *Sarah Palin Book Tour — Going Rogue in Cobleskill!* Climbing out of a Lincoln Town Car was the sensational best-selling author herself, former vice presidential candidate and political phenomenon of the decade, Sarah Palin. Ms. Palin had on a red miniskirt and blue sleeveless top and was wearing shades with white frames to complete the patriotic color scheme. Her big hair was more orderly than it normally appears on television, and both her calves and Adam's apple seemed to have grown. Otherwise, Ms. Palin was very much herself, chatty and vivacious.

Some McDonald's customers gawked and a few began to head our way, grinning and waving, but we had no time for public relations. Anyway, we had just ten copies of the Palin book that somebody had picked up at a discount at the Stuyvesant Plaza Book House, and we were saving those for the former mayor of Wasilla's biggest fans in Cobleskill.

Our motorcade made its way to the strip mall with Crafts-a-Palooza at one end and Subway at the other. I peeled away from the procession as it approached the Brienings' storefront and cruised around the back of the building and parked by the Subway Dumpster. Marylou called my cell, and we kept our connection open so she could keep me informed as to everybody's location in front of Crafts-a-Palooza.

One of Marylou's crew out in the parking lot had a bullhorn and I could hear it all the way in the back of the building when he began to announce: "Come and meet Governor Sarah Palin! Meet the woman who wants to help you take back your country! Read her great book full of good ideas and big words and mavericky attacks on liberals! Come and get your Sarah Palin tome, and meet the next president of the United States!"

Marylou's voice said into my ear, "People are starting to come out of the store. Some are walking down from Subway, too."

"Have your guy with the speaker keep saying Palin's name until the Brienings appear." I had explained to Marylou that the Brienings were a small ferret-like couple. I hoped that this wouldn't be the day when six other small ferret-like couples happened to be shopping at Crafts-a-Palooza and they all raced out to meet Sarah Palin while the Brienings remained inside the store because they were hard of hearing and would miss their opportunity to meet their sociopolitical goddess.

The bullhorn kept blazing away, noisily hectoring people for half a mile around to gather by the Palin van and meet the famous political personage and now best-selling author. I was poised by the metal back door of Crafts-a-Palooza with my lock-picking tools and, if I had to use it, my crowbar.

Marylou said, "Here come Clyde and Arletta. They look excited."

"I'm going in."

The lock was easy, and there was a bar inside the door that I used the crowbar on. I was inside the Brienings stockroom and office within a minute. The lights were on and I headed for their desk, an old wooden job with a dusty desktop computer on it and a couple of file cabinets next to it. I didn't see anything that looked like a lockbox. I had asked Timmy what a lockbox was, and he said I would have to ask Al Gore.

The Crafts-a-Palooza stock room smelled terrible, and my throat started getting scratchy. I guessed it was the potpourri. There were huge crates of it nearby, shredded dead vegetation treated with an assortment of chemicals, most of them toxic, I guessed, if not lethal. If I hadn't had a more urgent task, I would have phoned the EPA.

I saw no safe — my chief worry had been that the Brienings had a safe that was locked and too heavy for me to carry — and I didn't see any "box" either. The file cabinets were unlocked, and I began flipping through the manila folders. There was nothing filed under Van Horn or Rita or confession or embezzler.

"What's happening?" I asked Marylou.

"There are fifteen or twenty people. The Brienings are trying to elbow other folks out of the way."

"Slow them down if you can."

There was a wooden crate nearby with what looked like old financial records heaped atop it. I flipped through these, fruitlessly, and then set the records on the floor and lifted the lid off the crate. It was full of more reeking potpourri. I replaced the lid and set the bank records back where I had found them.

My eyes were watering and I sneezed. I sneezed again. Then I sneezed a third time.

Lockbox, lockbox. Where was the lockbox?

I opened the drawers of the desk, but they were full of office tools — scissors, staples, rubber bands — and junk mail from the Republican National Committee. Hanging on the wall above the desk were various "awards" from the RNC for helping save America from socialism.

I went back to the file cabinets to see if maybe a "box" of some kind had been secreted behind the rows of stuffed file folders. Nothing. I had a brainstorm and decided to check the crates of potpourri to find out if a box had been buried inside the many pounds of leaves and twigs.

I opened one crate and sneezed again. Then again. Then I sneezed and sneezed and could not stop sneezing. The lavatory was nearby, its door ajar, and I went in still sneezing, and wadded up bits of toilet paper and stuffed them up my nostrils. But when I sneezed again one of the wads shot out my nose, and then the other one became dislodged and flew across the enclosure and bounced off the door.

I kept on sneezing, and I could only think, Christ, I've got to get out into the open air.

I managed to say to Marylou, "What's happening out there?"

"What?"

"I'm sneezing. What's going on with the Brienings?"

"Oh, darling they wanted to buy a dozen books, but now they are acting…odd."

"Are they — *atchooo* — suspicious?"

"I think they might be. Especially Arletta. Clyde is plainly in love with the governor, but even he is starting to look at her in a funny way."

I sneezed some more, and Marylou said, "What? What?"

My eyes were watering so badly that I was having a hard time seeing the Brienings' desk or anything else. I wiped my eyes with my hankie, but then the sneezing started again and the eye watering got even worse.

I said, "I have to get outside. I can't see. Or breathe without sneezing."

"Somebody is talking about calling nine-one-one," Marylou said. "Arletta said something about imposters. I'm afraid they're onto our merry chicanery, Donald, luv."

"Then pack up and leave. I'm heading out. If I can find the door."

"Are you all right, darling? Oh my."

"Leave the books in the parking lot and go back to McDonald's. I'll meet you all there."

"We sold all the books. Clyde and Arletta bought six. Raphael autographed them."

I sneezed some more but managed to wipe the tears from my eyes long enough to get out of the Crafts-a-Palooza back door and slam it shut. I got my car going and barely missed the Dumpster behind Subway. As I pulled around to the front of the strip mall I could make out through the blur of tears the Palin book tour van and the Lincoln Town Car cruising out of the parking lot and onto the highway.

Back at McDonald's, I went into the lavatory and washed out my eyes and sneezed some more and cleaned myself up as well as I could with a fistful of napkins I had grabbed.

Outside, the book van, its sign removed, had left for the drive back to Albany, but Marylou was waiting and looked worried about my well-being and appearance.

"Donald, you look like Olivia De Havilland in *The Snake Pit*. Is Hunny going to have to have you committed?"

"I didn't find the so-called lockbox. Or anything else. I was attacked by crates of potpourri. The Brienings might as well have had a rottweiler in there."

"A little potpourri goes a long way. I have a quarter of an

ounce or so in a Burmese lacquer dish in my Palm Beach boudoir, and it is more than enough to clear my sinuses after a long day of doing charity work."

My cell phone went off, and it was Hunny.

"Donald, girl, how did you make out snatching the lockbox?"

"I'm sorry to say that I wasn't able to find it. My information turned out to be too vague, and I didn't get lucky."

"Oh, well, rats. Antoine didn't have any luck either. Mom and Tex weren't at the Lake George Super 8 either, and the desk clerk wouldn't tell them who was staying there. They checked the Silvery Moon again also, and they are all heading over to Cobleskill now to meet Quentin and the other RDQ boys who are on their way to Crafts-a-Palooza. They're going to perform an exorcism on the crafts store, they said. I told them not to bother, really. But they wanted to help out in the way they know how. And what harm is there in it, anyways? They should be over there any minute now if you want to watch."

CHAPTER TWENTY-SEVEN

Marylou rode with me in my car, and we parked along the highway about a hundred yards from the crafts store. Hungry and worn out, we had picked up a couple of Big Macs and a bottle of water at McDonald's and sat and ate while we waited for the show to begin.

"Oh, I've never eaten one of these before," Marylou said. "This time of day I am generally pecking at a ladylike nibble of fois gras."

"Are you enjoying your burger?"

"It tastes predigested. As if it had been marinating in someone else's stomach chemicals."

"If you say that, you are arguing with success."

"I wasn't criticizing, just pointing out."

We chatted for a while about Palm Beach life and about the Saratoga social scene during the summer racing season. Marylou reminded me that Rita Van Horn had also been an aficionado of the race track, and this gave me an idea as to where Hunny's mom and her friend Tex might have been spending recent days, if in fact it was her old pal from Texas who had carried Mrs. Van Horn away to parts unknown.

At seven nineteen, the Radical Drama Queen convoy arrived. The strip mall lot was nearly empty, except for three cars in front of Crafts-a-Palooza and four or five down at Subway. There were no cops around. The Brienings apparently had not reported the fake Sarah Palin book event, and they must not yet have discovered that the lock on the back door had been broken and their desk and files rifled.

Shoemaker's little Fiat led the way, and it was followed by what looked like a twenty-year-old Ford Econoline van, and then Antoine's Chevy Malibu with the twins and two of the RDQ boys in it.

"Well, won't this be fun!" Marylou said.

"Yes, and if you want to join the party, go ahead. I think it's better if I stay out of it to minimize the chances that the Brienings will connect this with Hunny."

"I hate to go dressed like this. But I don't want to miss out either. So tood-lee-oo, Donald. I'm sure I can ride with the RDQ ladies if it becomes necessary to beat a hasty retreat. And if Clyde and Arletta recognize me as Sarah Palin's publisher's rep, I'll just tell them I've gone all mavericky like my boss."

Marylou had another swig of water and then strode across the tarmac to the RDQ crew, who were out of their vehicles now and were decorating themselves with objects they were lifting out of a number of what looked like burlap sacks. The August evening light was weakening now, but the parking lot lights were coming on automatically and I had a clear view of the proceedings.

The exorcists dressed themselves not in Christian priestly garments but in feathers and what appeared to be fresh vegetables. Some wore pole bean vines with the beans dangling, and others cherry tomato vines. A couple of the RDQers draped themselves with floral wreaths, daisies and day lilies and cosmos and zinnias. One wore a vest that seemed to have thousands of M&M candies glued to it. Two wore the saffron robes of Buddhist monks, and it was they who brought out from the van several sets of drums and some smaller objects that were too small for me to identify from my vantage point.

Antoine and the twins were in attire that was normal for them. Antoine wore jeans, a big Mexican blouse and his long rhinestone earring. Tyler and Schuyler were in shorts and T-shirts with big pictures of bare feet on the front, in anticipation perhaps of their careers as podiatrists.

Shoemaker himself, in his Brooks Brothers shirt and Jack Wrangler necktie, had a bullhorn in hand, and it was on his apparent signal that the group formed an arc around the entrance to Crafts-a-Palooza and immediately began drumming and chanting. I could hear ringing and tinkling too, and I soon saw that many of the exorcists were ringing Buddhist prayer bells and somebody had a triangle and another cymbals. Davenport the astrologer appeared with a conch shell and began to accompany the various percussionists with mournful lowing sounds from his sea horn.

The men swayed back and forth in front of the crafts store, and as they did so people began to trickle out of the store and out of Subway to see what was going on.

It was then that Shoemaker lifted his bullhorn and began to recite: "We freemen of all colors of the spectrum, in the name of God, Ra, Jehovah, Anubis, Osiris, Tlaloc, Quetzalcoatl, Thoth, Ptah, Allah, Krishna, Chango, Chimeke, Chukwa, Olisa-Bulu-Uwa, Imales, Orisasu, Odudua, Igzeahbeher, Kali, Shiva-Shakra, Great Spirit, Dionysus, Yahweh, Thor, Bacchus, Isis, Jesus Christ, Maitreya, Buddha, and Rama do exorcise and cast out the evil which has taken hold of Crafts-a-Palooza and of its human-form proprietors Clyde and Arletta Briening. Clyde and Arletta are inhabited with demons of greed and incredible rotten meanness, and in the name of all the gods of the universe and the municipality of Cobleskill and the state of New York, we cast those satanic entities OUT! OUT! OUT!"

Now the drums began to beat faster and the bells to clang and jingle, and as the exorcists swayed with the rhythm of the percussionists, they all shouted along with Shoemaker, "Out! Out! Out! Out! Out, demons, out! Out, demons, out!" Davenport blew on his conch shell, and now many of the RDQ men began to repeatedly lift their arms heavenward, as if to hoist the strip mall into the air. Plainly they intended to levitate Crafts-a-Palooza, and make it shake its evil spirits out of the structure, the way the thousands of National Mobilization to End the War in Vietnam protestors tried to shake the demons out of the Pentagon in the fall of 1967.

I spotted no evil spirits spurting through the roof of Crafts-a-Palooza into the evening sky, but I did see several customers exit and trot toward their cars, and they were followed outside by Clyde and Arletta Briening. The Brienings stood goggle-eyed outside their store's front door. Clyde had his glue gun in hand, and Arletta brandished a cell phone that she seemed to be barking into.

Some people ambled down from Subway to watch the spectacle from a distance, and others pulled in off the highway.

Some of the exorcists kept up the chant of "Out, demons, out!" while others took up a new refrain now, "Hari, hari, hari, hari, rama, rama, rama, rama, Krishna, hari Krishna, hari, hari, rama, Krishna."

Now a flashing cop car pulled in, a local Cobleskill cruiser with a lone officer at the wheel. He moved slowly toward Crafts-a-Palooza, apparently puzzling over this probably unprecedented scene outside a Cobleskill strip mall. He halted thirty or forty feet from the exorcists, left his flashers on, got out, paused, then walked toward the Brienings.

The RDQ boys kept up their drumming and clanging and chanting and their so-far unsuccessful attempts to cause the mall to rise shuddering into the air.

As the cop spoke with the Brienings, another vehicle pulled in, a van. A man with a videocam got out and immediately began recording the occasion. I guessed he was the local stringer for one of the Albany or Schenectady TV stations.

The television videographer's timing was to prove significant, for it was soon after his arrival that Shoemaker included in his exhortations some specifics that turned out to have serious consequences. Hollering into his bull horn, Shoemaker let loose with, "End the greed! End the cruelty! End the persecution of Hunny Van Horn. The demons inhabiting Crafts-a-Palooza and inhabiting Clyde and Arletta Briening must be exorcised, must be sent flying away, must be stopped from stealing Hunny Van Horn's billion dollars that he legitimately won in the New York State Lottery…"

Shoemaker went on in this vein for a couple of minutes, maybe trying to make the cop see that if he interfered with this sacred ritual he risked incurring the displeasure of a celebrity.

The Brienings were now yakking at the cop a mile a minute,

Arletta waving her cell phone, Clyde aiming his glue gun. The cop then stepped aside and made a call of his own.

Five minutes later, with the strip mall still refusing to rise off the ground and the exorcists drumming and chanting and trying even harder to make the damn thing budge — at least an inch — two more police vehicles drove in off the highway, one of them local, the other a State Police cruiser with four officers in it.

I figured it was a good time for me to melt away.

CHAPTER TWENTY-EIGHT

"Donald, I do like the way we live our sedate lives," Timmy said. "But I have to admit that when I look at these Radical Drama Queen guys and at Hunny Van Horn and his colorful entourage, I feel almost Mormon. Have I turned into Mitt Romney without even noticing it?"

"Yes."

"After all these years, are you going to dump me for a man wearing farm produce?"

"No. Shh."

We were in the bedroom on Crow Street watching the Channel 13 eleven o'clock news. The Cobleskill strip mall exorcism was the lead story. The theatrical ritual had pushed the holdups, house fires and state legislator scandals that generally dominate local news coverage back several minutes. This was because the Crafts-a-Palooza event was surprising and because some great visuals were available and because of the Hunny Van Horn connection. Quentin Shoemaker's blunderingly connecting Hunny to the exorcism made it all extra newsworthy. Shoemaker had told me by phone afterward that he was sure his mentioning Hunny would engender both public and spiritual support for Hunny. But the predictable downside was about to become evident.

After a couple of minutes of footage of chanting, drumming and unsuccessful attempts to levitate the strip mall, Shoemaker was interviewed briefly. He again accused the Brienings of trying to steal Hunny's billion dollars, though without mentioning how they were hoping to pull off this dastardly feat.

Clyde and Arletta were interviewed next, and after some tea-bagger-style rhetoric about socialism and Obama's satanic minions, Arletta said that yes, it was true, that Hunny Van Horn owed them half a billion dollars, but after today's disruptions and insults they felt that the entire billion ought to be turned over to them to compensate for their pain and suffering.

Arletta concluded, "And if we don't have the money by noon tomorrow, we will be calling a press conference and making an announcement that Hunny Van Horn will not be pleased to hear the contents of."

Timmy said, "Uh-oh."

"Yeah. This is bad."

A Cobleskill police official was interviewed, but only briefly. He said that when the exorcists were threatened with arrest for disturbing the peace, they agreed to pack up and leave only if they were first allowed to stick daisies in the cops' rifle barrels. The police sergeant had explained to Shoemaker that they didn't have any rifles with them, and anyway it wasn't the '60s anymore and if the RDQers knew what was good for them they would move along. Which they soon did.

Next came an even briefer live report from a reporter standing somewhat forlornly outside Hunny's house on Moth Street. She said that Hunny was inside the house and had sent word out that he would have no comment on the Brienings or anything else that night.

Then the Channel 13 anchors moved on to a water main break in the town of North Bethlehem.

"Hunny is screwed," I said. "I let him down."

"Maybe his mother won't even care all that much about the embezzlement revelation. If she's even alive. Didn't you say her mind was slipping?"

"Oh, she's alive, I think. I'm confident her pal from Texas and a guy named Herero have her somewhere. They may be on their way back to Texas, for all I know. If they were around here, by now they'd likely have heard that Mrs. Van Horn is officially a missing person, and cops and volunteers are searching for her in fields and culverts up and down the Hudson Valley. The chances are good the three of them are in a Motel 6 in Chattanooga on the way back to Houston, or maybe holed up in a casino in Connecticut. Would she care about the embezzlement revelation? That's hard for me to say. Hunny says yes, the Van

Horns are respectable Christian people who would be crushed by the charge. But I'm convinced that that's the case only with Hunny's sister and her husband and Nelson and Yawn."

"Isn't it Lawn?"

"Lawn, yes."

"Surely the DA isn't going to make a big deal of a charge coming so late in the game. How long has it been? Ten years?"

"Thirteen."

"There might be statute of limitation problems for the prosecutors. It's not murder we're talking about here."

"Murder might be better. It's racy. It's tragic. It's deeply human. Embezzlement is merely embarrassing. And except for Hunny — who has made a career of being the exception that proves the rule — the Van Horns apparently loathe social embarrassment more profoundly than anything else on earth."

"It's almost refreshing to discover social shame in a family," Timmy said. "You don't have to be a Muslim jihadi to regret that the near disappearance of shame in American life is a serious social loss. Puritanism is one thing, *The Bachelor* something else."

My cell phone rang, and it was, as I thought it might be, Hunny.

"Did you see the news?" His voice was barely audible.

"I did. I'm sorry, Hunny."

"Can you come over?"

"Sure."

♫ ♫ ♫ ♫

On Moth Street, the security guys were still on the front porch and two TV crews were on the sidewalk dozing on collapsible chaises. Inside, Marylou and the twins were in the living room watching a true-crime channel. Hunny and Art were at the kitchen table.

"Where are the Green Mountain Boys?" I asked. "Have they returned to Mother Earth's bosom up north?"

"Those hippies sure did turn out to be royal pains in the neck," Art said. "They went ahead and ticked off the Brienings, and now those ass wipes say they want the whole billion dollars. And Hunny is seriously considering giving it to them."

Hunny was chain smoking by the evidence of the overflowing ashtray as well as the deadly haze in the room, and he had a bottle of Jack Daniels and a half-empty glass on the table in front of him. "Quentin and the boys are good-hearted lads," Hunny said, "and they mean only to be helpful."

"The road to hell," Art said, "is paved with good intentions. Those guys are jerks. All those drums and crap."

"Be that as it may, their hippie habits didn't stop you from helping yourself to a little of that boy Ethan. You had no complaints about drums along the Mohawk when you were chewing on that comely lad's cute member last night."

"I'm not saying they weren't friendly. Just stupid."

"Well, what's done is done. Yes, Donald, Quentin and his drama queens have departed for Vermont. They had to go back and milk the chipmunks or something. And in a sense what they did tonight it is just as well. Perhaps it is all part of the Lord's plan."

"How so?"

Hunny sipped his whiskey and savored its return to his life.

"I am just sick to death of the whole Instant Warren so-called bonanza. Everything was just fine for Artie and myself until that so-called good luck fell on me like a ton of bricks. Yes, I needed to pay off the Brienings their sixty-one thousand dollars. But I still have to pay them, and now they want the whole kit and caboodle billion dollars. And all I'm left with is a lot of people mad at me and Mom missing and nothing to show for my so-called good fortune except a lot of sorrow and tears. Plus, of course, the billion dollars, for the moment, which is nothing to sneeze at. Anyway, Nelson called right after the news was over and they think I should offer the Brienings nine hundred million and see if they will take it. Miriam is adamant about it not getting out that Mom is a crook."

I said, "Well, you would still have a hundred million, a fortune. But you're sure you don't want to tell the Brienings to just shove it and let the chips fall where they may? The DA is unlikely to go after an old lady in a nursing home with a failing memory."

"No, but it's people's opinions. All the other Van Horns besides myself have always been respectable. Respectability sucks as far as I am concerned. I'd rather not be — what did Quentin call it? — some boring old assimilationist. But people should get to choose for themselves. I got to choose who I got to be, and Miriam and Nelson and Lewis and even Yawn should also get to choose who they want to be. It's only fair."

"Hunny, you are a kind man," Art said. "Even to your relatives."

"So," Hunny said, "here's what I would like to do, Donald. Please accompany me tomorrow morning out to Cobleskill. Let's see if the evil Brienings will take nine hundred million. That would leave me with enough to give a million each to thirty or forty of the nice folks out at the warehouse — not including Dave DeCarlo — and also pay off Stu Hood his thousand and even Mason Doebler his thousand. Plus put the twins through medical school, and replace the tires on the Explorer, and a few other odds and ends. And if the Brienings won't accept that deal, then fuck 'em — they can have the whole billion. Just so they give back Mom's confession and promise in writing never to bother her or me again. And I would go back to work at BJ's, and I would see if I can get my pretty darn good life back the way it was before the skies opened up and started raining shit."

Art said, "Instead of men."

There was a long, sad silence.

"I'm so sorry, Hunny," I said, "that I was so little help to you."

"Oh, you've been a godsend, Donald, in so many ways. Except for one little thing you don't seem to be willing to go along with, even in return for your fat fee."

"Well, I'm glad I haven't been a total disappointment."

"I think you need a drink."

"I don't care for the hard stuff. I just never developed a taste for it. But I wouldn't mind a beer and sitting out on the front porch with the security guys for a while and relaxing. It's such a nice night out."

Art brought some cold beer up from the old fridge they kept in the cellar, and we went out with Marylou and the twins and sat on the porch steps and watched the bugs throw themselves maniacally against the streetlights.

CHAPTER TWENTY-NINE

I thought I heard drumming but soon realized it was someone banging on the door of Hunny and Art's guest room. I had locked the door and gone to sleep instantly after two bottles of Sam Adams, but now it was six twenty Wednesday morning and Hunny was pounding on the door yelling, "Donald! Donald, girl, wake up!"

"Huh? Coming."

"It's Mom! They found Mom, and we're going to drive up and get her."

"Oh, good. Where is she?" I yanked some pants on and opened the door.

"She's at the Super 8 in Lake George. With Tex Clermont, just like you said. And that Mexican."

"Great."

Hunny was in his boxers and sleeveless undershirt and was red-eyed but animated. He said, "One of Tom In Paine's people nailed her and called the cops, so I guess we can't hate Bill O'Malley and those terrible tea-baggers too much."

"I guess not. Is coffee made? I'll be down in a minute."

"There's one other thing though, Donald." Hunny lowered his eyes and his head got a little wobbly.

"Is your mother all right?"

"Yes, it's not Mom. That Albany police detective called. He wants to talk to me. To you, too. He's coming over, so we have to get out of here before he gets here. I just want to hug Mom before I have to deal with anything else."

"What's the problem now? Is it the Brienings?"

Hunny looked at me queasily. "Yes and no."

"So, what happened?"

"Crafts-a-Palooza burned down overnight."

"Oh. Oh my."

"The TV news says the police think it was arson."

"Oh."

"The whole mall went up in smoke and is totally destroyed. Subway too. Though they think it started at Crafts-a-Palooza. Both in the front and back."

"Right. Was anybody hurt?"

"No. A fireman got scratched or something."

"At least there were no injuries or deaths. The Brienings weren't in there, were they?"

"No, they were at home."

"Well, at least there's that."

"Are you thinking what I am thinking, Donald?"

"Sure."

"Will we have to tell the police?"

"I think so."

"I hate to. Stu is just a fucked-up kid."

"I know, but he could kill people again."

"I almost wish the Brienings were in there. I thought of what their little charred corpses would look like. But then I felt ashamed."

"I guess now they'll really be on the rampage. But we'll deal with them. The important thing is that your mom is okay. Let me get dressed and then we'll head up to Lake George. Is your mother in police custody?"

"Yes, her and Tex and Herero. Can I just have a hug before you put your shirt on?"

I hugged Hunny and kissed him lightly on the nape of the neck. Then he turned and clomped down the stairs and I headed into the bathroom.

ſ ſ ſ ſ

During the hour-plus ride up to Lake George, my cell phone rang four times. One call was from Timmy, who asked if I had heard the news. I said I sure had. The three other calls were form Lieutenant Card Sanders, and I didn't answer those. The messages he left, each one in a more urgent tone than the last, demanded that I contact him immediately. Poor guy. Dealing with celebrities could be such a hassle.

Hunny had spoken with Nelson, who was also en route to Lake George, and with his sister Miriam, who was terrified that the Brienings might not wait to be paid off but might just call the DA and announce to the world that Mrs. Van Horn was a "lowlife."

Art said, "Maybe you could get Stu Hood to burn your sister's house down, Hunny. With her in it."

"Artie, luv, don't say that. Miriam is a bitch, but she is family."

"I'm so glad I am an only child. Mom and Dad had me, and I guess then they said maybe we could do better, but let's not press our luck."

Hunny had learned from Nelson that the renegade oldsters and their pal Herero were at the Lake George police station, and my GPS led us there directly. An old Dodge Dart with Texas tags was parked out front next to two police cruisers, and Hunny said, "That clunker must belong to the Mexican."

We were led into a small conference room that smelled of stale coffee, and no more than a minute after we were seated there was a commotion in the corridor and two uniformed officers led an older, wrinklier, female version of Hunny into the room.

The cops politely went out and closed the door behind them as Hunny leaped to his feet and yelled, "Mom! Mom!" and grabbed the old lady and kissed her on one cheek and then the other cheek and then the first one again.

"Oh, Huntington, what a surprise this is! I'm having such a fabulous time, Hunny, and it's so nice that you and Arthur could pop in and share it with us. We've been having *soooo* much fun! I never thought I would have this much fun again — stuck in that stinky old home — but Tex and Herero rescued my bored-to-tears old bones for this little vacation from old age, bless their hearts."

Mrs. Van Horn was gotten up in a chic box-seat-at-Saratoga outfit, beige silk slacks and top, pearl earrings and a Texas-style big-hair do that in no way resembled the old-lady perm in her photos. The hair-do may have been the reason no one recognized her before Tom In Paine's snitch zeroed in on the Golden Gardens runaway.

"But Mother Van Horn," Art said, "Hunny was so worried about you, and so was everyone else."

"Mom, folks have been looking high and low for you. You didn't tell Mrs. Kerisiotis you were leaving, and everybody has been scouring the countryside looking for your corpse. Mom, you have given us all a terrible scare, you little dickens, you!"

"Oh, Lord, did I forget to call Golden Gardens and say I'd be away for a few days? It must have slipped my mind. You know how forgetful I've gotten. Oh, for heaven's sakes, I do apologize if I caused any bother."

"But didn't you see yourself on TV? It's been all over the news that you were a missing person."

"Oh, I guess we weren't watching that channel. Tex and I watch QVC. I don't know why Herero didn't see that. He watches the news, plus MTV and boxing. Hunny, you know I never liked looking at the news. It is so depressing. I like *The Golden Girls* and shopping. I don't buy, just look, for the most part. But Tex got some nice jewelry, some fling for Herero and a couple of nice things for me, what I've got on. I forgot to bring clothes, you know. Tex had things sent overnight right to the Super 8 were we were staying in our very nice room."

"I think you mean *bling*," Hunny said. "Now, Antoine and the twins and this psychic from Vermont looked for you at the Super 8, but they didn't see you anywhere."

"I guess we were out sightseeing, maybe riding around on the paddle boat. Or over at that nice restaurant with the stuffed haddock."

"Where are Tex and her friend now?"

"Tex is in the lady's. She'll be crawling down here in a minute or so. Herero must be waiting for her. He is so good to Eileen. It's not easy for her with her walker at the track, but Herero got her a wheelchair to get us from the parking lot to our seats, and he went and placed our bets."

"What track? Saratoga?"

"You know, Hunny, Nola Conklin had her TV on last week and there was this announcer saying the races were going on, and I got to missing the track. I did used to love the ponies. So when Tex called, I just said, why don't you ride up here with that nice young aide who wants to marry you, and we'll have a few cocktails and a nice time for a week or so, and then we'll go back to rotting away in our old folks homes. Well, Tex just leaped at the opportunity. Tex has her daughter down there, but she never comes to see her, not like Hunny. Nola told me you had won a lot of money in the lottery, Hunny, so I figured I could hit you up for a tenner if need be. But I never wanted to be a burden, and I don't intend to be. Anyhow, Eileen is well fixed. She is an extremely generous friend."

"Oh, Mom, that whole lottery thing has turned out to be a total pain in the butt." Hunny introduced me and said, "Donald is a private detective who has been helping me deal with all kinds of shkeevy types that have crawled out of the woodwork since I won a billion dollars. Blackmailers, swindlers, what have you. Even the you-know-whos in Cobleskill are bedeviling me and trying to get hold of my money. Mom, I was better off middle-class, believe you me. Anyway, if I have any money left after all the headaches have been cleared up, I'll give you a million dollars. Or ten million, whatever you need."

"Thanks, Hunny. You have always been such a good son. I have enough for my needs, but you could help Herero if you feel like it. He saw on the news in Texas about your prize. He's afraid his muffler is going — it does make quite a racket — plus he has some lawyer bills for something. His papers, I think."

"Is he nice? He sounds nice."

"Herero is very sweet. And I think he might be…you know." Mrs. Van Horn flapped her wrist once.

"Well, I am putting Herero down for a mil. Not to worry. But…well, there is a problem, maybe, with the money. The you-know-whos in Cobleskill are demanding a billion to pay them to continue to keep their mouths shut about you-know-what."

Mrs. Van Horn glanced over her shoulder at the closed door. Through the glass we could see one of the cops standing in the corridor. She said, "You know, they sent me another threatening letter. At Golden Gardens."

"I do know that. And guess what? Now they're probably even madder than ever at you and me. Last night their store burned down."

"Oh, good heavens!"

"It's a smoking ruin, television said."

"Maybe my you-know-what letter burned up. But probably not. I think they kept it in the lockbox with the other books and the other money."

I asked, "What other books and what other money, Mrs. Van Horn?"

She gave me a wary look, but Hunny said, "Mom, Donald knows all about everything. He is an understanding man with a Christian soul who is one hundred percent on our side. I'm thinking of giving him thirty million dollars as a bonus if everything turns out okay. So you can tell him anything."

"Well," she said, "it's the second set of books Clyde and Arletta keep for Crafts-a-Palooza that the tax people aren't meant to get a gander at. And the cash they skim off at the end of the day. That's how I was able to help myself when I went through that crazy spell after Carl passed. They had about a million and a half in there, and if I had a bad day at the track I would just help myself once in a while. Except, Arletta got suspicious, I think, when I told her I was betting the house on a horse called

Epworth Lady and that nag didn't even show, and the next day I was right back at the track. She counted the money, and she nailed me. It was my terrible downfall that we've all been paying for ever since, and I admit that I did wrong and my comeuppance was earned."

Art said, "The Brienings are also crooks, it sounds like. Holy crap."

"But Mom," Hunny said, "if they were blackmailing you, why didn't you blackmail them right back? Good grief, it sounds like they are even bigger miscreants than you are."

"I thought about that. And I did finally get up my nerve to say something. But Arletta said that what they were doing is what everybody does, and what I did was stealing."

"Oh, Mom, you got taken for a ride. We all did. Those Brienings are nothing but scum."

"Where is the lockbox located?" I asked. "The box with the confession, the second set of books and the large stash of currency?"

"The lockbox was always buried under some potpourri. It's at the bottom of a big crate called Elvira's Herbal Kisses."

I glanced at Hunny, who caught my look, and then I excused myself and walked out into the corridor, past the waiting Lake George officer, and out to my car. I phoned Card Sanders, and before he started in on me, I explained a few things to him and urged him to get hold of the state fire marshal's office immediately. He listened with care, heard what I said, and agreed to make some fast calls and then get himself over to Cobleskill to help search for the lockbox.

Sanders said, "I'm relieved to see that Mr. Van Horn is likely to come out of all this with both his fortune and his reputation intact. Unless, that is, it was Huntington himself or somebody he hired who set the fire at Crafts-a-Palooza. That would put a much darker slant on the situation."

"Yeah, well, we can talk about that. I have some information about the fire that you'll be greatly interested to hear, Lieutenant."

I gave him a quick rundown on Stu Hood, and how Hood had both a history of arson and a powerful personal interest in not letting the Brienings take away all of Hunny's lottery winnings. I told Sanders where he could probably find Hood after the place opened in the early afternoon, and then I rang off and walked back inside the police station.

Tex Clermont and Herero Flores were in the conference room now with Hunny, Art and Rita, and everyone was chatting away and guffawing, and wrists were flapping, and I came in just as Hunny yelled at Herero, "You go, girl!"

Herero, short and pleasantly round-faced with a fuzzy little goatee, shrieked and said, "And you wouldn't believe the tat on this lifeguard I met at the beach down from the motel!"

"Not Sean Shea!"

"Yes, he said he knows you and he said maybe you gonna give him a million dollars, just like you gonna give me!"

"Sure, why not!" Hunny sang out.

"Oh, I just knew this would all work out," Tex Clermont said grinning. "I knew y'all would just hit it off like y'all was old bosom buddies, just like Rita and yours truly." Draped over a folding chair, her walker parked next to her, Tex was a good six feet tall, with shining blue eyes, eight pounds of rouge, and a heap of hair like the fake Sarah Palin's at the Cobleskill book party.

Hunny said, "I don't know what's going to happen tomorrow, but I have to tell you this. Today is the happiest day of my life. To have my beloved mom back with me and to see her wonderful old friend and to meet her fabulous new friend is just the banana split with the cherry on top. I am blessed, and we are all blessed. And now why don't we all go somewhere where we can count our blessings and…have a few celebrationary cocktails!"

Everyone in the room shrieked except me, although I had to smile too. The cop outside in the hall turned and looked through the glass at us, and he also looked pleased with the way things were turning out.

CHAPTER THIRTY

The Lake George police were too smart to swallow any of the "reality show hoax" guff that the tea-baggers were spreading. The cops bought Mrs. Van Horn's unlikely but true story that she and her pals were just off having a break from nursing home life. They said they would notify both Golden Gardens and Tex Clermont's assisted living facility in Houston that the ladies would be back in a matter of days and "the gals" would get in touch themselves when their plans were clearer.

Nelson and Lawn soon arrived in Lake George, and they joined us for lunch at Joey and Bernie's Take-a-Peek Inn, the place with the good stuffed haddock.

"Grandma Rita," Nelson said, after we had ordered our fish platters, "we can certainly understand why you would want a break from nursing home life, even from such a comfy-cozy place as Golden Gardens. But next time, why don't you just phone Mother or me? It would be our pleasure to take you out for a steak dinner at Jack's. And maybe even a cocktail or two." He winked.

"Yes," Lawn added. "You are very dear to us, Grandma Van Horn. It would be our great pleasure to be seen in public with you."

"Oh, that is so sweet. You boys make such a nice couple. You know, I'm so glad there are so many gay boys in our family. Boys who really know how to have fun. Not a bunch of stick-in-the-muds like most Van Horns have been."

Nelson blushed and Lawn quickly scanned the room to see if anyone was listening.

Tex said, "Yes, you gay boys are *baaaad*. And I think we can see plenty of evidence of that right at this table. Herero, honey, you can barely keep your eyes open. I know you were out tomcatting around all night because I heard you come in next door at four fifteen a.m. You know, I left my Zolpidem in Houston, so I sleep very poorly."

"Oh, Tex," Hunny said, "I can get you some pills. The twins have a regular pharmacy in their bike bags. They're two young friends of Artie's and mine who plan on practicing medicine. I'm putting them through podiatry school."

Nelson and Lawn exchanged glances, and Lawn reached for the bread basket.

Herero did look droopy-eyed, but now he perked up and said, "I haven't yet completed my education. But Hunny is gonna help me out, too."

"What are you studying, Herero?" Art asked.

"Nursing. I'm pretty good with the TLC already, but I need more skills and the piece of paper."

"You can TLC me anytime, Herero," Hunny said gaily, and everybody guffawed except Nelson and Lawn.

"Uncle Hunny, we're out in public now," Nelson said.

"You're right, Nelson," Mrs. Van Horn said. "We're not locked up in the old folks' dungeon today, so I guess I can't tell any rude jokes, either."

Tex said, "Well y'all can play goodie-goodie if that's what y'all want to do. Me, I'm too old and too bowlegged to care. Now, Nelson. Did you hear the one about the lady and the supermarket bag boy?"

"Oh, Tex, you old devil, you," Hunny said. "That joke is not for tender ears like Nelson's."

Art said, "You could change it to scratchy Toyota."

Tex, Rita, Herero and Hunny howled over that one. Nelson and Lawn looked perplexed, but neither asked for a clarification.

The stuffed haddock lunch went on in this jolly vein until, as coffee was being served, my cell phone rang, and I walked out to the parking lot to take the call.

"I've got good news and semi-bad news," Card Sanders said. "The good news is, I was there when the fire marshal located the lockbox, so-called. It was at the bottom of the remains of a burned wooden crate that may well have contained the dead-leaf smelly stuff you described to me. The contents of the lockbox, however, were charred. The box was not airtight and the material inside combusted. There appeared to be the remains of paper documents and what the inspector said were crumbled bits of U.S. currency. Quite a bit of it, in fact."

"That's the semi-bad news, I take it. So, what's the good news, Lieutenant?"

"Clyde and Arletta Briening were on the site when we recovered the lockbox and its contents. Asked about it, they claimed they had no idea what it was or how it had gotten there. They said maybe the arsonist left it to confuse the police. They said there had been a break-in earlier in the day, and their back door had been pried open."

"Uh-huh."

"That's bullshit, of course. But with nothing to go on but Mrs. Van Horn's unsubstantiated allegations, the DA isn't likely to want to send the charred papers to the state lab for a time-consuming and very expensive forensic analysis. The upshot is the Brienings are out their million-plus dollars in unreported income, and the Van Horns are free of any charges or accusations the Brienings were intending to make against them, whatever those charges and accusations might have been. I'll bet you know what those charges and accusation were. Am I right?"

"Sure."

"Both Clyde and Arletta told me they don't like the Van Horns — they called Hunny a degenerate fruitcake — but as far as that family is concerned they're willing to let bygones be bygones. They said they were glad to hear that Mrs. Van Horn had been located and that she wasn't dead at the bottom of a quarry, as they put it. And now they just want to concentrate on collecting the insurance money and rebuilding their store, they said."

"Sounds good."

"They do, of course, want the arsonist caught and the crime

prosecuted."

"Yeah. He should be restrained. That I can't argue with. The guy could really hurt somebody the next time."

I only wished that the priest who had raped Stu Hood when he was a child and probably wrecked his conscience and filled him with loathing could also be locked up, maybe in the same state prison. But that wasn't anything I or Sanders could do anything about for the moment.

I went back inside the restaurant and announced to Hunny and the others that the Brienings had been neutralized and both Mrs. Van Horn's good name and Hunny's billion dollars had been saved and were now secure.

Hunny said, "Well, I am so relieved that those wicked cretins in Cobleskill are now off Mom's back. Now, Mom, no more bezzy-wezzy for you. Promise?"

"Bezzy-wezzy?"

"Hand in the till. You know?"

"Oh, my word, I forgot all about that tomfoolery. It was so long ago. I can't remember what I did last week, for heaven's sakes."

Art said, "So, Hunny, you get to keep the billion dollars. We could have made do without it, but you have to admit that it's sure to come in handy."

Hunny looked pensive. "The billion dollars is actually more of a burden than I really want to shoulder. It has brought me mainly grief, and I almost wish I had never bought my Instant Warren tickets and then won that gosh-darn prize."

All eyes at the table watched Hunny anxiously, including mine. Lawn's mouth was actually hanging open.

"But," Hunny said, "if some tired old fart like Warren Buffet can put up with being a billionaire, I guess I can, too."

"Yes, Hunny, be brave," his mother said. "You can do a lot of good in the world with that amount of money. Help the less fortunate, spruce up Moth Street at Christmas with loads of pretty lights."

"Support education," Herero said. "You already said that."

"And of course if you invest wisely," Nelson said, "you can increase your considerable assets substantially."

"Nelson, you are on the money with that sound investment comment," Hunny said. "And I have only one word for you — all of you gathered here who may end up with a piece of my big yummy money pie."

"What's that?" Tex said. "I hope it's not playing the ponies like your mother." Tex and Mrs. Van Horn looked at each other and snickered.

"Is the word *plastics*?" Art asked.

We all leaned in to listen to Hunny's one-word investment strategy. "Oh, Artie, who do you think you're talking to? Am I Hunny Van Horn, or am I Hunny Van Horn? The investment word has got to be *Applebee's*!"

Hunny did buy over eight hundred million dollars' worth of Applebee's stock, enabling the restaurant chain to expand into such locales as Lock Haven, Pennsylvania; Bethel, Maine; and Addis Ababa, Ethiopia. At the company's annual meeting, Hunny was elected to the board of directors. He and Art toured many of the franchises. They were popular visitors, although they were asked to leave Utah following an incident with a bus boy whose fake ID misstated his actual age.

Hunny gave away many millions of dollars to his former co-workers at BJ's Warehouse. Most of the recipients used the cash to further their educations or fix up their homes, although several also became addicts and drunks and got into gunfights with other family members.

While the twins' grades at HVCC were not good enough to get them into a pre-med program, Hunny helped them open a foot massage parlor at the Crossgates mall in the space the Brienings had been planning on expanding into.

Hunny never heard from Clyde and Arletta Briening again. They rebuilt their Cobleskill Crafts-a-Palooza store with the insurance money from the fire. They remained active with the Family Preservation Association of Albany County and other tea party groups, but they did not make any major donations to any of them. Bill O'Malley did not return to Albany and didn't mention Hunny again, although he did include in his show a brief approving mention when the Brienings got their own reality show on Bravo, *Arletta, Get Your Glue Gun!*

Marylou and Antoine, who each received five million dollars from Hunny, quit their jobs at Golden Gardens and the tax department and often traveled with Hunny and Art, where they handled corporate communications and media.

I never received a bonus of thirty million dollars from Hunny. That apparently slipped his mind. He did, however, give me a nice tip of four percent on my regular fee. He told me the tip would have been much larger if I had played my cards right, and we both had a good laugh over that.

For several months, Rita Van Horn had her own elegant Albany apartment overlooking Washington Park, complete with live-in staff. But she was bored, she told Hunny, so she moved back out to Golden Gardens. The Willett Street folks didn't laugh at her jokes, she said. Hunny paid for Tex Clermont to leave Houston and move in with Rita at Golden Gardens. Nola Conklin moved down the hall.

Nelson and Lawn were given a million dollars each of Hunny's money to invest as they saw fit. Lawn put all of it in "bundled habitable-shelving securities" in Tokyo, and it vanished as soon as Japan's economy began to recover.

Mason Doebler received one thousand dollars to get his Pontiac fixed, but no more, and he dropped his frivolous lawsuit after Bob Chicarelli, Hunny's lawyer, pointed out to Doebler's lawyer that the combination of Doebler's assault convictions and his scary appearance would work against him with a jury.

Stu Hood received his thousand also. The day after we all returned from Lake George with Rita Van Horn safely in tow, Card Sanders and I spoke by phone.

"Strachey, you misled me with this Hood guy. He has an arson record, yes. Burned down his folks' house with them inside it. Grisly. Horrible. But he did not do the Crafts-a-Palooza fire."

"He didn't?"

"The fire was set between two and three fifteen in the morning. Firefighters were on the scene by three forty. Hood was stinko at the Watering Hole, that gay bar on Central Avenue, until closing time at four. Twenty people saw him there, including the two bartenders, and most of these people strike me as credible witnesses. So he didn't do it. He wasn't surprised that he was a suspect. He was just pissed off. But Stu Hood did not do this crime. Repeat — did not. Any other ideas?"

I thought about suggesting that Mason Doebler be questioned.

But I figured that that would be a waste of time and unfair to Doebler.

Then I remembered who it was who badly wanted to get hold of a piece of Hunny's billion-dollar boodle and who had traveled over a thousand miles in a dilapidated automobile in order to do so. Someone who had been barely able to stay awake after "tomcatting around," as Tex Clermont had theorized, until after four a.m. on the night of the fire. But was this some kind of ethnic profiling on my part? And what was the evidence? No, it felt too amorphous even to mention, too much of a reach.

I told Sanders, "I'm at a loss. Dozens of people are going to profit from Hunny keeping his billion dollars and the Brienings being shut out. I can give you a list. But as to where to start, it beats me, Lieutenant."

He grunted. He never believed a word I said, and I felt bad about that. He was an honest cop, and I was a lying creep asshole jerk realist.

I found out later that Herero Flores got his million from Hunny but apparently did not attend nursing school. Tex Clermont learned that Herero took off for Mexico soon after his return to Houston and no one knew exactly what became of him. Someone told Tex that Herero had a sometimes boyfriend in Acapulco, a butch top reputed to be a mob enforcer who burned down businesses that refused to pay a percentage of their gross income to the local godfather. Tex's eight-carat diamond wedding ring turned up missing, and she suspected that Herero had made off with it. But she said she couldn't be sure, and anyway he was such a loveable little lady-boy.

On Labor Day weekend, I drove Timmy up to Lake George to show him some of the Hunny Van Horn-case attractions. We stayed at the Super 8 Motel, the one the Radical Drama Queen psychic told us Mrs. Van Horn was holed up in.

"Some people do seem to have amazing intuitive powers," Timmy said. "I'd guess, though, that it was just a motel chain the guy had heard of and the name popped into his head."

"But why not TraveLodge? Or Days Inn? Or Holiday Inn Express?"

"Are you saying that Mrs. Van Horn's aura possibly drifted down from the Super 8 and into this guy's brain?"

"Maybe. Her energy field. Look, if Verizon can make speech and thoughts fly through the air and land in somebody's head, why can't the human brain do the same thing? It's electrochemical after all."

"It can't for the simple reason that the human brain is not as well organized as Verizon."

"Maybe some people's brains are. Just not yours or mine."

"Donald, you're giving me the heebie-jeebies. You're going all hippie on me again. I'd half expect you to turn up with flowers in your hair — if you had enough hair left to stick any flowers in."

"At least I don't have hair growing out of my ears, like you."

"Ha ha."

"Or my butt."

"You love that I'm getting hairier. Admit it. Even as you become less so."

"That reminds me. I want to show you what I'm told is an amazing sight."

We walked down to the beach, asked around, and found Sean Shea, the lifeguard. When I identified myself as a friend of Hunny, Sean was plenty excited — this was a celebrity-contact-once-removed — and he agreed to show Timmy and me his tat when his break started in forty minutes.

Afterward, as we headed over to Joey and Bernie's Take-a-Peek Inn for lunch, Timmy said, "It was a poor likeness. It looked more like Dick Cheney."

"Yes, but that's not the point. It is a brilliant act of defiance. It's that impudent, tasteless, fuck-you part of gay culture that I am afraid is going to disappear as so many of us toodle off to the altar and register our decorating choices at Georg Jensen or

Sears. It's why I value Hunny Van Horn even though I wouldn't dream of living a life so rude and messy and even dangerous as his."

"I admit, Donald, that you're right to value the cockeyed caravan of Hunny's style of gay life. In my head, if not in my wussy viscera, I do too. So. Are you going to get *your* dick tattooed? Not an image of someone you can't stand, like that Sean guy did, but maybe a likeness of one of your cultural heroes? Gabriel Garcia Marquez? Thelonius Monk?"

"No, I think you should go first. How about Saint Augustine? Or the entire masthead of The New York Review of Books?"

He laughed. "Sure. I could get them all on there. Could you?"

RICHARD STEVENSON is the pseudonym of Richard Lipez, author of twelve books, including the Don Strachey private eye series. He also cowrote *Grand Scam* with Peter Stein, and contributed to *Crimes of the Scene: A Mystery Novel Guide for the International Traveler.* He is a mystery reviewer for *The Washington Post* and a former editorial writer for *The Berkshire Eagle.* Lipez's reporting, reviews, and fiction have appeared in *Newsday*, the *Boston Globe, The Progressive, The Atlantic Monthly, Harper's,* and many other publications. Four Don Strachey books have been filmed by here!TV. Lipez grew up in Pennsylvania, went to college there, and served in the Peace Corps in Ethiopia from 1962–64. He is married to sculptor Joe Wheaton and lives in Becket, Massachusetts.

THE DONALD STRACHEY MYSTERY SERIES

Print ISBN# 978-1-60820-013-9
Ebook ISBN# 978-1-60820-014-6

Print ISBN# 978-1-934531-97-6
Ebook ISBN# 978-1-934531-98-3

Print ISBN# 978-1-60820-090-0
Ebook ISBN# 978-1-60820-091-7

Print ISBN# 978-1-934531-97-6
Ebook ISBN# 978-1-934531-98-3

Print ISBN# 978-1-934531-33-4

Print ISBN# 978-1-60820-009-2
Ebook ISBN# 978-1-60820-010-8

MLRPress.com

Stimulate yourself.
READ.
www.manloveromance.com
THE HOTTEST M/M EROTIC AUTHORS & WEBSITES ON THE NET

CPSIA information can be obtained at www.ICGtesting.com
Printed in the USA
LVOW12s2151010913

350536LV00001B/16/P